AN ANCiƐNT HⱰWL

COMPILED BY

DIⱰNE NⱰRRⱰWⱰY & MⱰRISHⱰ KIDDLE

Edited by Toni Glitz
glitzedit.co.uk

Cover image by Ron Miller
ISBN: 978-1-916756-08-3

Veneficia Publications
December 2023

VENEFICIA PUBLICATIONS UK
veneficiapublications.com

TRICK OF THE LIGHT
Sam R Geraghty

Trick of the Light
The silent moon peeks
from behind innocent clouds,
like a murderess
that loiters in night's temple.

She strikes wildly,
eerie in her vindictiveness
she is the hangman,
passing a virgin
to the mouth of a wolf.

She laughs at the tears
shed in her name,
blesses the saliva
borne of crooked teeth
whilst other celestial
guests
refrain,
till the light dims out,
the universe to vanish
and play no more of
her game.

EXTRA SENSORY CHEMISTRY
Royston Fowler

Nosedive to oblivion!
Floating on air
Swirling surrounds
Like clouds, but not there.
Animal engines roar!
Silently deafening the daily drudge:

Rotating
Revolving
Vibrating
Exciting
Imaginatively, enlighteningly evolving.

Blue sky to black
White moon, stars shine
Sweet breeze, cool touch
Warm feeling.

Time passes but what force is real?
Blood on flesh, rust on steel
Colours collide. Shapes merge
The world runs on ... and away.
Machine grinds, motion begins

A first revolution:
Cogs click
Amaze!

Labyrinth's path
Climb!
Becomes clear.

Haze of daydreams and nightmares crash
Fear and life fills
Drowning?
Breathing!
Tangled
A web, caught in the trap.
Reaching, stretching
Touch!

Electrical bond
Arc weld
Seconds to minutes.
Sound and sight, drifting in a sea.
Chemical
Physical
Biological.

CONTENTS

In a world filled with tales of fantastic and legendary beasts, I wonder if werewolves aren't just the darker side of the deadliest creature of all—humans.

Tread quietly.

BERTRAM BROWN
Diane Narraway

Bertram Brown, or Bertie as he was known, had, he believed, led a fairly miserable and boring childhood. For a start, he hated his name. His older brother was named Jackson— Jackson Brown had a ring to it, and his friends called him Jax. Jax was, unlike Bertie, a cool name. Jackson had been named after Jackson 5, his Mum had been a massive fan, and his parents had met at a Jackson 5 tribute night. His mother had grown up in Fossil, Oregon— the other source of Bertie's misery. Fossil, Oregon is a ridiculously small town populated mostly by old people. Bertie had one friend, Billy Jones, but even with a friend there was nothing much to do.

Of course, Bertie complained regularly to his parents, but complaints about his name were always met with the same response.

"You have a fine name. You should be proud. You're named after your great uncle, Bertram Westover. He was a bit of a celebrity around here you know?"

It was a rhetorical question, and Bertie had the same eye-rolling response, every time. Of course, he knew, he'd heard it ever since he could remember. Betram Westover, had been a writer for the local paper. In a town populated by a little over 500 people, how could he be anything other than a local celebrity? He, Bertram Westover, had died the day Bertie was born, and Bertie hated him for it. He wasn't proud of his name in the slightest, and he cared even less about Bertram Westover.

His parents had both lived and worked in New York City, but once Jackson had come along they had upped sticks and moved back to his mother's hometown, Fossil. They had used their savings to buy one of the handful of hotels in the town, and Bertie was never going to understand what had possessed them to do so. Jackson joked that it was named Fossil because it was largely populated by the elderly. Bertie didn't find any of it amusing. He found the whole thing tedious and miserable. As soon as he was old enough he would definitely leave Fossil and probably change his name. He was undecided about the last bit, as grown-ups seemed less bothered by having stupid names than children.

It was Bertie's 10th birthday, and as a treat his dad had taken him and his friend, Billy, to Bear Hollow for a camping trip. This was something Bertie did enjoy—the highlight of his year.

This year began the way his birthdays had begun for the last couple of years— breakfast, followed by a couple of small presents: a trapper hat and the latest X-Men

DVD, Wolverine. His dad cooked pancakes, and then they set off for their camping adventure.

The day had been busy and both boys were exhausted, it was a beautiful night, but sleep was the top of their agenda.

"I need a pee," mumbled Billy.

"It's Bear style I'm afraid boys," grinned Bertie's dad.

"What?"

"You know, in the woods, Billy." Bertie laughed, heading for a small clump of trees.

He had positioned himself nicely behind a tree, still in shouting distance if needed, and was just reaching down to open his fly when he heard a twig crack behind him. This was instantly followed by the sound of leaves rustling, and breathing. Bertie was frozen, unable to either move or shout. He held his breath, but the rustling grew nearer and just to the left of the tree he saw two large yellow eyes. He tried to scream but no noise came out, just a stream of warm urine, which trickled down his leg. The yellow eyes now had teeth and he could clearly see that it was a wolf and it was heading straight for him. Bertie managed to scream just as the wolf sank its teeth into his arm, tearing at the flesh. He drifted on the edge of consciousness, partially due to the pain but mostly due to fear. Bertie's dad reached for his rifle and raced to help his son. Billy had been oblivious to this but as soon as Bertie had screamed, Billy had too, and passers-by rushed to assist as the two boys' screams echoed around the woodland.

Bertie's dad fired a couple of shots and managed to scare off the wolf, which had sunk its teeth into his youngest son.

"Billy! Billy! Get my phone from the tent. We need to call for help."

It seemed an age before help arrived but eventually it did.

"Perhaps it was a werewolf. Better keep an eye on him next full moon," joked a young paramedic, trying to make light of Bertie's injury. "It seems fairly superficial Mr Brown, so shouldn't take too long to heal. Perhaps next time take a gun with silver bullets—I mean you never know." The paramedic winked at Bertie, and he managed a weak smile.

It was only a couple of hours before they left the emergency room and headed home. Both boys sat on the back seat in silence.

"Looks like you'll get your main present early this year." Bertie's Dad smiled.

"I guess so," replied Bertie, managing to smile back.

"It is pretty cool," whispered Billy, and Bertie nodded in agreement.

This was the most exciting thing that had ever happened to anyone in Fossil. He almost couldn't wait to regale Stevie and the rest of the kids at school with tales of his bravery. And who knows, perhaps it was a werewolf.

Despite his hopes of turning into a wolf, the full moon came and went, and nothing.

It was shortly after Bertie's 13th birthday, by which time all talk of his wolf bite had long since subsided and the only evidence it had ever happened at all was a small scar on his left forearm. He could hear the wind outside his bedroom window whistling softly through the trees. Over the next few hours, the storm increased. It had been slow to come but eventually the rain lashed against the glass, and the wind howled through the trees. Bertie pulled his covers tight around him, just the sound of the storm made him shiver, and as the moonlight streaked in through the window he felt a tingling sensation in his fingers. He looked down and his nails had grown—significantly. They were longer, darker, and pointier. Hang the storm, he leapt out of bed, put the light on and took a closer look. They definitely looked like claws. He fumbled around for his torch as best he could with claws, turned the light off, and got back into bed. Once safely under the covers he switched on his torch and waited for what came next. What came next was absolutely nothing—zilch, nada—and he eventually fell asleep.

The following morning there was no sign of the claws, and he wasn't entirely sure it hadn't all been a dream, or hallucination brought on by the storm. However, just in case anything else occurred, Bertie thought it best to be informed.

Following breakfast, he headed to Fossil library, such as it was. He came away with everything he could find on werewolves: the twilight series, a couple of erotic otherkin novels, and one on lycanthropy, which he gradually worked his way through. Once he had completed them, he got more serious—the internet. Any books that featured werewolves in any capacity he literally read cover to cover. If nothing else, he would be an authority on werewolves. The librarian had concerns about some of the more adult content in these books and promptly phoned his mother.

"Oh, well, at least he's reading something," his mother mused.

"But Mrs Brown, some of the books he took are, well, a bit racy. Are you sure it's suitable?"

"I'm sure it's just a healthy phase, I wouldn't worry. Boys will be boys."

The librarian wasn't especially reassured but decided it wasn't worth wasting her time worrying about it. If his mother was OK with it, who was she to argue?

7

The following full moon he grew claws again, and after that he grew pubic hair. Two months later, sure enough, the claws appeared and that month there was a blue moon. It was on the blue moon that the familiar claws were accompanied by excess hair on his hands. Nothing, but nothing, in any book had prepared him for this. It didn't matter because he knew enough to know this wasn't normal and sooner or later he would change completely, and there was a very real possibility he might well bite some poor unsuspecting child on a camping trip.

Three months after his 14th birthday, on the night of the full moon he felt the claws grow on his feet as well as his hands. This was followed shortly after by his voice beginning to change. He knew this couldn't go on indefinitely. Sooner or later, he would change completely, and what then? What if he bit his mother or father—or Jackson? Or one of his friends? He didn't really know which was worse, and anyway he didn't really want to bite anyone. All this gradual changing was nothing like any of the books he had read. He was no heroic Twilight werewolf. There was no underlying animal magnetism that girls found irresistible, and as for the erotic novels, they were just plain silly. He stared at the claws on his hands and feet, and the hairs on his hands, which seemed to grow thicker each month. He made up his mind that he would leave home

8

before the next full moon. Sure, his family would worry about him, but that worry was nothing compared to the fear they would experience when he completely changed.

It was late June when Bertie left home. He packed some clothes and some food out of the kitchen. The bonus of living in a hotel was well stocked cupboards and large, equally well stocked fridges. At 3am on the 24th of June, Bertie Brown left his home and family and headed out into the night. He had no idea where he was headed, but woods, forests, mountains were all possibilities—anywhere people weren't.

He'd only been gone a day or two when the full moon rose high above the dense woodland, he ate the last of the bread and cheese, and stashed his backpack in a nearby ditch and waited. The gradual changing was an inconvenience but something he had no control over. On this occasion he watched the claws and hairs grow on his hands and feet. It didn't hurt like in books or the movies, in those they were nearly always wracked in pain or writhing in agony. He felt neither of those things, just anger at having to leave his home and family, and fear of the dark, what may be lurking in the woods: more wolves, bears, cougars, rattlesnakes, spiders, and of course human predators. He was scared and lonely and slowly changing into a werewolf, whatever form that may take. He had no idea whether he would look like a wolf-man or an actual wolf, or something completely different. He did know however, that his current predicament was all down to that damned wolf bite four years previously. He hated that damn wolf.

Once the sun had risen, and he had returned to normal, he trudged through the woods and tried to resign himself to this new life. This was not an easy task, but the camping trips as a young child had made him slightly more resourceful than he may otherwise have been. Days turned to weeks, his food ran out and he had precious little money as it was. Eventually he came across a cabin.

There are a few types of cabins secreted away in the woods: the trapper's cabin, where trappers spend hunting season; the hunters retreat, where hunters spend the occasional weekend; the family holiday home, or those owned by rich men as a weekend getaway with the mistress. Then, there are the cabins lived in by those who have opted out of society. The latter was the least desirable, and of course, was the one he found. This particular cabin was inhabited by a dead recluse, several rats and not much else. It was small with no interior plumbing, but it was shelter and fortunately the corpse hadn't been a corpse long. Also, there was a stream nearby to get fresh water and plenty of logs for the fire, which doubled up as a stove.

Bertie didn't care who the corpse was or how he had died, just about getting rid of him. He had to bury or burn him, that much was obvious: burning him might attract too much attention, so burying him seemed preferable. It took a few days for him to dig a deep enough hole, meanwhile he wrapped the corpse in old blankets and a mouldy looking tarpaulin. There were plenty of animal furs so sacrificing a couple of blankets seemed acceptable. Eventually, whoever the corpse had been, was laid to rest.

Once that was dealt with, and as many rats as possible evicted, Bertie considered his new life. He was alone but at least now he had shelter, a gun, some shells, and traps. He was in with a fighting chance of survival. He didn't have a dog, they always had a dog in the movies, but he thought perhaps it was for the best—he might eat it come the next full moon, which didn't seem like a good thing. There was a truck though, not that he could drive, but how hard could it be? Most useful was money, so if he failed at hunting, he could at least drive to the nearest town and buy something. He was far enough from people to go through metamorphosis without too much disruption to anyone. He decided, too, that he should change his name. James Logan seemed good—after the

Wolverine. James Logan was a much better name than Bertie Brown.

The moon rose high and full on his first transformation in his new home. He had taken to getting undressed at sunset as the change would damage his clothes. There was no pain as such, just a strange numbing sensation as he gently morphed into a wolf. He was not a grotesque wolfman or a gargantuan musclebound wolf-like creature, he was simply a wolf, like any other wolf—like the one that had bitten him: a beautiful wolf with yellowy, hazel eyes, four oval toes and a soft grey coat.

He ran through the woods, feeling the late summer earth beneath his feet and the cool night air on his face. There were so many scents, it was hard to decipher each one, but his wolf instinct took over and he pursued his prey, in this instance, a rabbit. He licked his lips satisfied by the raw flesh and tang of its blood. He tasted the air; it tasted fresh, tinged with the last hint of rabbit. This was his first night as a fully-fledged wolf, and it was exhilarating. He wondered if there were others about and he howled. He wasn't certain if he wanted to be part of a pack, but he definitely felt the call of the wild. He caught the scent of a deer and gave chase but on this occasion it eluded him.

    With the first light of the sunrise, he
gently morphed back into a 14-year-old boy
with a stubbly chin and breaking voice, not that
there was anyone to talk too. In truth it was a
lonely existence, his body was changing, and he
had no one to talk to about it, and the
metamorphosis which had caused him such
angst was now all he looked forward to. The
freedom of running wild through the forest,
irrespective of the weather and howling in the
clear moonlight, those were his best times.

    As he grew older, and his needs changed,
he found work on one of the nearby farms. He
also began to frequent some of the closer towns
more, where he would visit the whorehouses or
streetwalkers. That was where his money
went—on food and women. He had no need for
booze, his needs were purely physical: lust and
hunger. He was a good enough trapper and
forager, but bread and cheese tasted good and
were beyond his capabilities. Physical comfort
too was something he craved, but not love. Love
would be too complicated, and what if, when
the moon was full, he hurt his wife or children?
Wasn't that why he'd left home in the first
place? To protect those he loved. It was on one
of these full moon nights that everything
changed.

    The moon was full for the second time
that month and he had sensed it coming and
was sat naked outside in anticipation. Sure
enough, he changed into a wolf. There was a

13

gentle breeze ruffling his fur and the evening scents filled his nostrils. This time, there was a new scent, one he hadn't noticed before, one he felt compelled to follow.

He heard the howl as it drifted on the breeze and caught the scent of another wolf, and not just any lone wolf, this was a she-wolf. James, as he was known now, had been living alone in the woods for around 6 years, and had never so much as heard a faint, distant howl, and now suddenly there was another wolf nearby. There was no way of knowing how much ground he covered, but eventually he caught up to the lone she-wolf that was permeating his senses.

He stopped when he saw her, there was no human interaction, just wolf instincts. The ritual between this wolf and his mate was like any other. He didn't think she was beautiful; he didn't desire her in the way he did the women back in the town. He didn't think she had lovely eyes or a wonderful smile. She smelt right and she obviously sensed he did too. There was no thoughts in either of their heads; there was just animal magnetism—a need fulfilled by an action.

He awoke just after sunrise and made his way back to the cabin, naked and as such vulnerable. He felt satisfied but wondered at the consequences of his actions. He was grateful the she-wolf was not there when he awoke and that he didn't encounter her on the way home, as he wasn't sure she would recognise his scent as a human. Was his behaviour last night acceptable? He was, after all human, and sex between humans and animals was both perverse and illegal. He threw up. Something he had never done before following a full moon escapade, but then he had only ever been alone in the woods. He briefly entertained the thought that she might be like him; it stood to reason there must be some others like him out there, for a start there was the one that bit him. He hated that wolf! And it would be a cruel irony if he had just mated with that particular beast. Surely, fate could not be so cruel. It was at this point he realised, that despite his extensive research, there were things he still didn't know about werewolves. Things that couldn't be known unless you either were a werewolf or knew one.

He assumed, or rather concluded, that all werewolves were probably lone wolves, in much the same situation as him; living as reclusive humans in order to protect those they love. For some, he felt, this may have been a hard lesson to learn, but sooner or later they would have outcast themselves to more remote, sparsely inhabited regions. How long the average werewolf lived was something else he didn't know. Most wolves only lived 16 years, whereas humans lived anything up to hundred plus years. He was 20 now, incredibly old for a wolf but young for a human. He didn't feel old, he felt strong and healthy, virile even. Perhaps werewolves aged more like humans, they were human most of the time so that made sense.

He returned his thoughts to the previous night. It wasn't great sex he was reflecting on; it was sheer animalistic needs. It was necessary at the time, but he cringed at the grotesque thought of baby wolf pups with human appendages or heads. And what if it happened again? Would he slowly populate the woodlands of America with these grisly looking hybrids? He threw up again, before heading into town. He had never tried strong drink, but he had seen plenty of others drink away their sorrows. So, he reasoned liquor might work, at least long enough to get some sleep. It took a quarter of a bottle of cheap whiskey before James lost his capacity for any thought.

A couple of full moons had passed and there had been no sign of the she-wolf. James was not sure whether to feel relieved or lonely, and to some extent he felt both. The day was crisp and bright and although the first snow of the winter lay on the ground, the sun was shining. James had only just taken his first sip of coffee when the door knocked. Nobody had ever visited him, and he was afraid his family may have found him, something he was totally unprepared for. On the one hand of course, he would love to see them, while on the other he would have to do more explaining than he was willing to. There was a second knock and James briefly crossed his fingers before slowly opening the door. His heart was pounding, and his palms were becoming clammy, and by the time he opened the door he had convinced himself that whatever lay on the other side was not going to be good: his parents, the police, angry farmers, disgruntled townsfolk. His list was endless, with no possibility of what or who was actually knocking.

When he finally opened the door, he saw a pretty young woman holding a baby in her arms with three pups following on behind her.

"Hi, I'm Donna, and this little bundle is Tala. May we come in?"

THE WEREWOLF WHO WOULD NOT
Kathy Sharp

Once upon a time there was a werewolf. Not your common or garden werewolf, you understand. This one was wayward in the all the wrong ways, and though he loved his mistress, the Moon, he disobeyed her and tried her considerable patience again and again.

What did he do, you ask? Well, it wasn't what he did that caused the trouble, it was what he didn't. He was the werewolf who would not. He would not howl; he would not snarl and slaver; he would not terrorise the local people by chasing them about the forest and the farms; but most of all he would not bite and create new werewolves. Didn't like the taste, or so he claimed.

Even for the patient Moon, it was very trying. After all, she gave him, once per month, the freedom to indulge the animal side of his nature. In return, he would hunt, and chase and create fresh werewolves. It was a simple exchange of services. But this werewolf never fulfilled his side of the bargain. There were times, indeed, when the Moon threatened to take away his wolf-nature, return him to permanent mortality, for repeated breach of contract. Each time he wept and begged for just one more chance.

"Very well," she would say, against her better judgement, "one more month. More fool me!"

For all this, the Moon loved her wayward werewolf, and he loved her. So you see, it was a relationship fraught with contradictions.

The werewolf, for his part, did not take her threats lightly. He had no wish at all to return to full mortality. He loved his mistress, the Moon, and wanted to please her, but he loved being a wolf more. He loved running through the forest on four legs. The lupine movement was almost fluid; he flowed round tree trunks, dribbled under low branches, washed through brushwood, all unstoppable. And as he went, he quoted mortal poetry. Tennyson was good. It was an absorbing, enchanting way of being, and he spent his dull days as a mortal dreaming of it. The chasing and biting, on the other hand, was unpalatable, nasty, brutish, and the werewolf with the poet's soul wanted no part of it.

Then one night, he was loping through the woods, brim-full of happiness, quoting Tennyson—the one about the Lady of Shalott. He had just got to the dramatic bit where the mirror cracks, when in front of him he saw his worst nightmare. A small lost child, rooted to the spot, staring in terror. The werewolf stopped and stared back.

"Come," he said kindly, "it's dangerous here. There are werewolves about, you know. Let me see you out of the forest."

The child heard only a frightful growling and rolled himself into a ball.

"Please," persisted the werewolf. "Go away. Shoo. Or I shall be compelled to bite you." The child moved not at all.

The Moon, looking down on this scene, slapped a cloud across her face in exasperation. What was she to do with this werewolf who wouldn't? Her patience was finally exhausted.

"Bite him!" she snapped. "He cannot escape. He expects it! I expect it! Do it!"

The werewolf stood up on his hind legs, man-style, and looked sadly at the Moon, as she glittered icily among the branches, showing her true colours at last.

"I would not," he said. "I would not harm this child for all the world. Not even for you."

"Very well, so be it," said the Moon.

She had a vengeful streak, and the werewolf was slowly and painfully transformed into a tall, purple-flowered plant. The werewolf could not speak or move. He was rooted to the spot as surely as the lost child had been.

"There," said the Moon. "I wash my hands of you. You are Wolfsbane now—a wicked poison to all—to man, to child, to wolves and werewolves, too. This is your punishment for repeated disobedience. Bad people will use you to poison their enemies, and you will poison the

21

unwary with no more than a nibble of your leaves. You would not bite—but now you will kill those that bite you. Quite appropriate, don't you think?"

And the Moon gave a spiteful smirk, and turned her face from the werewolf who would not.

THE ISLAND
Kay Matthews

I loved my little sister; I would kill for her. There had been times where it had almost come to that. Everywhere we'd lived, people seemed to have taken against her, scurrying away from her as we walked through the streets, whispering in groups, making strange symbols with their fingers. Those were the easy people to deal with. There had also been bands of young men who had shouted at her, called her names, and thrown stones. Those were the people I'd come to blows with. At those times I'd lost control, it was like a dark grey mist descended, and I couldn't remember a thing afterwards. I'd come back to a silent world, covered in blood, the persecutors having fled ... my little sister staring at me silently with her big green eyes, blood on her lips.

In my 15 years on this earth, we've lived all over the island of Aurelandis, from the base of the snowy peaked mountains to the sculpted bronze canyons of the Nayal Valley in the East. There was just me, my sister Lissie and our mother, Kara.

Kara and I looked alike: we had dark brown hair, cornflower blue eyes, and warm brown skin. Lissie looked completely different: her eyes were huge and bright green; her hair was fiery red, and her skin was pale. Her teeth were sharp and pointed. Maybe that's why everywhere we went she was met with suspicion; there was no one else who looked like her. Or perhaps it was because at 12 years old she was yet to speak. She communicated to us with gestures. She spent time making symbols on the ground with a stick, there seemed to be a pattern in the marks that she made, and she looked at me as if she was trying to say they meant something.

At other times she was in her own world, humming to herself or rocking slowly, curled tightly in a ball, like a little animal. She would rescue insects from drowning, she would nurse an injured mouse back to health. Dogs were drawn to her, cats hissed and ran, like most of the people we encountered. She only responded to me and Kara. I adored her completely, she was my sweet and loving little sister, and I would die for her.

After the last incident, Kara got us to pack up and leave in the night. We trudged for miles across heathland and bog until we started to climb higher, and the landscape turned to short grass and grey boulders. Our family loved a night-time journey, especially Lissie. She came alive in the light of the moon, it's like she was a different person; confident, strong, and wild.

We eventually arrived at a wooded glade and set up our camp. We used sticks and thick woven sheets to make our home. In the distance I could see wooden huts; the homes of people who lived in one place for time. I once asked Kara why we needed to be near other people, and she said that she'd tried living in isolation when Lissie and I were very young and found it too difficult. She said we needed other people to survive. She wouldn't answer any more questions after that. That's what Kara was like, she would answer one question only, as if it was the only question in the world, and it pained her greatly to create the answer. I asked about my father once, and got snarled at, so I did not ask again. All I knew was that Lissie and I probably had different fathers, and they were no longer around. Kara told the villagers that her husband was away seeking our fortune, or on a ship, or he'd stayed behind to care for our livestock—she had a new story each town we went to. Being a female with children without an adult male was frowned upon in Aurelandis, and Kara said it would make us more vulnerable than we already were.

We were not a usual family; I could tell that. I didn't think other families had the same rituals we had. For example, once a month I was forced to drink what Kara called medicine, in a special cup. It was a disgusting tasting substance, although she mixed it with sweet spices to try to mask it. I would drink it for 3 nights. I always fell into a deep sleep afterwards and woke up the next day feeling strangely tired and heavy. I did not ask her what the medicine was for; Kara did not answer questions, and you did as Kara said: the two universal truths of my childhood.

Anyway, in our new home, I started making friends. There were some nice people in the huts near our camp, they brought us food they had stored from the summer, and they seemed unconcerned about Lissie's unconventional appearance. As spring came, I started going hunting and walking with some of the children from the village. From talking with them, I started to experience how it would feel to live somewhere permanently, and I liked it. Kara said we could maybe stay, and we started to build a wooden hut. Lissie also seemed happy; she enjoyed decorating our new home with wildflowers and wooden carvings she'd made.

The summer brought heat and butterflies. We started inviting people round to the hut, cooking the fish we'd taken from the lake. I laughed often; even Kara almost smiled once. The local people pretended to believe Kara's tale that our father was at sea, but you could tell they knew we were on our own, and they didn't care. They embraced us tightly. I stopped worrying so much about Lissie, although Lissie remained somewhat silent and watchful. We had found our home.

One night, in late summer, Lissie and I were lying in a meadow near our neighbour's hut with a group of locals, and Kara came running up to us. She spoke to us quietly and urgently, saying it was late, we needed to be home, and I needed to drink my medicine. I was annoyed at being interrupted. I had grown larger and bolder and was starting to enjoy the company of my friends. Kara had started to appear older and less of a threat to me. I refused. Kara shouted, screamed, and begged, but I remained firm. She eventually led Lissie away. Lissie looked back, as if she was sad for me. I don't know why, I was becoming stronger, and it felt good.

My friends and I drank berry wine and talked into the night. The moon rose, and I felt stronger still. I felt so strong I could burst. What happened next was incredibly fast. My body twisted and turned. It felt as natural as a knife going through butter, it was that smooth. I didn't feel any pain or fear, I felt amazing. My arms shortened, and the joints changed direction. My face elongated and my ears rose to the top of my head and grew like pointed triangles. My body dropped soundlessly to the ground and grew thinner and longer, my legs became short and springy. I had thick grey fur all over my body, and my vision changed. I looked at the people surrounding me, and they moved in slow motion. It would be so easy to chase, jump, catch and rip their flesh. The thought of this made me feel so much pleasure. I crouched, ready to leap.

28

From the edge of the forest, I heard a sound. A red-haired figure came dashing out into the clearing and threw herself in front of the village children. Her big green eyes were wet with tears, silently screaming for me to stop. I hesitated for a moment, confused. Her eyes tilted upwards looking behind me. That's when I heard the shot.

I woke up on the wooden floor of a cart. I found out later that Kara had taken it from the village, and the people had let her, quietly keeping their distance. Lissie was sitting over me, tending to my arm which she was bandaging. Kara was talking. She said we were heading south to an island, where she heard there was a cure.

"A cure for Lissie?" I asked. Both she and Lissie looked at each other in astonishment.

After some time, Kara told me to pay attention, as she was only going to say this once. She told me that yes, Lissie and I had different fathers. Lissie was from a line of healers whose powers only stayed intact as long as they remained silent; I was from a different line: the lycanthrope. The medicine I drank once a month was wolfsbane; this and Lissie's powers kept me from changing into the wolf. Kara had got together with Lissie's father as he was a healer, to help me, and Lissie was an unexpected surprise. Lissie's father, however, had left, begging Kara to come with him, which she could not. He had left her with a device loaded with silver bullets, for emergency use, and she'd kept it hidden all these years, never wanting to use it but unable to throw it away. She had Lissie, who from a young age helped me, and there was no more need for me to be imprisoned during the full moon. At times, when Lissie had been unable to use her powers, for example, when she'd needed to run from the persecution of others, I had partially changed and had harmed people, that's why we had to keep moving. Kara said she shouldn't have been complacent, and she was now determined to get to the cure for me.

I could see the island in the distance, a glittering jewel, with steep cliff faces in view, and seabirds screaming and squawking up ahead as we boarded a small boat. By the time the sea was on all sides of me, I felt different, fully relaxed and calm for the first time.

"I think the island is the cure," I said.

"I think so too", said Lissie, her beautiful voice like the chiming of bells, her eyes shining as she hugged me, smiling deeply. As we approached the mainland, red-haired, emerald-eyed people came to greet us.

We stayed on the island, surrounded by Lissie's family, learning the ways of the healers, and delighting in Lissie's newfound voice. She never stopped talking, and she grew up and married a very powerful man. I did not marry, but I felt peace in my life on the island, knowing that the sheer density of healing folk made it impossible for me to become the wolf, and that my family and newfound friends were safe. I stayed until my human hair was grey, and I drew my last breath.

IVO
Diane Narraway

My story comes from a time before time was recorded. A time of hostile beasts and strong family bonds. I grew up a hunter like my father, and his father before him. At the time my story begins, my father was one of the most revered hunters and his smelting pot was almost legendary. I, of course, was his protégé and he taught me to forge spears and arrowheads, and together we led hunting parties and we always returned with food.

My mother and sisters, like most women in the village, grew crops, but unlike other women my mother was an exceptional healer. Our village was small and self-sufficient, and as such, we had no need to trade and rarely dealt with outsiders.

My story begins when I was no longer a boy, and childish pleasures were laid aside. As I approached manhood, my duties increased and I began to lead more hunts, forge spears, and gradually take over from my father.

It was at this time I remember noticing how beautiful my older sister, Aki was. In fact, I spent an awful lot of time mooning around after her, watching her as she bathed and alleviating my desire the only way I knew how—alone. I knew Aki could see me watching her

33

and I let her. I let her see everything and she did nothing to discourage me.

It all came to a stop when my mother found me watching my sister bathe. She did nothing at the time, and we, of course, were oblivious to her presence, instead she waited until we returned home and took me to one side.

"Ivo, my son, I have noticed over my years that although many take their kin as mates, the children seem weaker. I do not wish that for you. You are strong and healthy like your father in his youth. Look elsewhere for a helpmeet and breed strong beautiful men."

I nodded. I didn't really understand but I respected her enough to obey her wishes.

A few days later my father took me to the nearest village and arranged a union between me and their chief hunter's daughter. She too, was beautiful and I remember my father saying that at my age all young women are beautiful, and it is a wise man who learns to be content with just one mate. He hoped I was a wise man—I hoped so too.

My skill as a hunter and forger was welcomed by the villagers, and so I stayed with my mate, and was as content as any man could be. She was a beautiful woman, a talented home maker who gifted me two fine sons. Despite life being good, I still thought of my sister in moments of solitude. I suspect I knew, even as a young man, that she would be my downfall.

My sons were small, the youngest only a baby, when the cold weather set in, and I was hunting further afield. The harsh winter meant hunting parties were separating to cover as much ground as possible.

On this occasion I had been out hunting for the better part of the day when I heard footsteps nearby. I moved stealthily and hid behind a bush, and there she was, my sister. Aki was as beautiful as I remembered and more than that, she was naked. I was aroused and for a few moments I forgot the penetrating cold, my mate and my sons, as my desire for Aki took over.

The relief was quickly overshadowed, and my lust forgotten, as I watched my sister writhe and contort shapeshifting into a wild beast. A wolf.

She stood for a moment and sniffed the air. I was petrified, unable to move, almost hypnotised by the creature before me. She howled and lunged toward me. I was helpless as she tore at my leg, ripping the flesh from its bones. Then she stopped and glanced into my eyes before running into the night.

I was found as the darkness gave way to the day by another member of the hunting party who helped me back to the village. My mate made me as comfortable as possible before sending word to my mother.

"Oh, my Ivo, my son what has she done to you?"

"You knew?"

She bowed her head in shame.

"Your sister is my curse, and you were my blessing, but now I fear you too are cursed."

"Why am I cursed? I don't understand." I was in a lot of pain and my mother's poultices and potions weren't really helping much.

"When I was younger, I too was attacked by a creature just as you were, but because I am a woman it affected me differently. I was in the early stages of pregnancy with your sister, so while I was never afflicted, my unborn child was. Every month when the moon rises full, Aki changes into a wolf. That is my curse."

"But why would you be cursed with such a thing, you are a good person, you have healed many children. Surely there must be a cure for this too."

She shook her head, and I could see tears forming in her eyes.

"I haven't always been so good. I had gone outside the village looking for herbs to remove my pregnancy. Aki is only your half-sister; my brother is her father. At the time I was promised to your father, and I was afraid but my actions angered the Great Mother and so I was cursed. Sadly, there is no cure, I have tried many potions, but nothing works."

"So, what will happen to me? You said it was different for women but what happens to men?"

"When a man is bitten, he then becomes afflicted and changes every full moon, for that one night. I instructed Aki to take herself far from our village and yours but—"

"—the cold weather drove us to hunt further afield."

She nodded.

"What can I do?"

I had no idea what was going to become of me. Aki had ripped at my knee, tearing the flesh and breaking the bone, and it was unlikely that I would walk again unaided, let alone hunt. It looked as though once a month I would become a crippled wolf.

"If I am unable to walk properly, I will be a vulnerable wolf, left to the mercy of the hunters. I am truly cursed."

"My poultices and potions will prevent infections and can ease your pain but that is all. However, I have heard talk of a place in Albion, a henge where great healers gather. Perhaps you could go there when you can walk. It would be a long journey but if you are careful and hide out of the way once a month, you could get there."

"I could follow the trade routes, if I take gold with me that should buy me passage."

"I wish you luck my Ivo."

That was the last time I saw either my mother or my sister.

The villagers were good to my family and brought us food while I was unable to walk. Fortunately, this was only a week or so, as my mother's herbal remedies had been of some use, and I recovered quickly. In just one week I was up and about using a staff and was able to teach many how to forge spears, arrows, and other metal objects to adorn the villagers and honour the Great Mother.

The first full moon since Aki attacked me was approaching and with no explanation, beyond the need for solitude, I left home and travelled as far as I could from any village. I doubted I would be a threat to anyone, but I believed they may be a threat to me. I had filled my belly before I left in the hope that I wouldn't be hungry.

I will never forget that night. As the moon rose, I could feel a tingling sensation throughout my body, something akin to pins and needles. I remembered my sister, naked in the moonlight, and I stripped, grateful for a milder night. Slowly but surely the tingling gave way to an ache, followed by intense pain as my limbs stretched and cracked. Where once I had fingernails, claws burst through my skin, my jaw grew to accommodate my extended teeth. There was an uncomfortable itch as fur covered my new body. I could feel the blood coursing through my veins and my heart beat strong and loud, echoing in my ears. Eventually the pain subsided, the itching ceased, and I felt strong. I longed to run wild and free; I tried but my leg was still injured, and pain impeded me. I limped to the river I was thirsty, but more than anything, I yearned to see my reflection. The night was bright and still, and I could see myself clearly in the water, I was beautiful. I drank my fill and limped my way back to the cave, where I had left my human accoutrements. There, I curled up and slept till daybreak.

It would take me several weeks to reach Albion and several more to reach the Henge. I saw very few people on my journey and stuck mostly to the countryside and dense forests. On full moons I hobbled away and hid. If I was lucky, I might catch a hare. Mostly I hid in caves licking my wounds in the moonlight. I'm not sure I believed in a cure, but hope can be a powerful driving force, and I hoped if nothing else, that they could repair my knee. To be able to run free in the woods on full moon nights like Aki, that would be something wonderful.

It was a long and difficult journey, and I wished to be able bodied, to have been able to hunt, to run and to not be hungry. I was an old man long before I should have been. I cursed my leg, my lust, and my stupidity—it appeared I was not a wise man after all, but oh, how I wished I had been!

It was approaching the longest day when I first caught sight of the Henge. I watched in awe as the sun's rays danced across the stones, and how they rose high into the sky, twinkling in the morning sunlight. I will never forget those moments; it was a formidable sight, far beyond the capability of any man I had ever met. As I stood there, I couldn't help but wonder if the stories I had heard as a child—of the fae or djinn—may be true, or if perhaps the Great Mother had built it herself. If the latter was true, I wondered what those who lived there had done to deserve such an honour, such an act of love. For the first time I truly believed that perhaps those who lived there were great healers, and if I was ever going to find a cure, it would be there.

"Beautiful beyond words, isn't it?" My silence was broken by a man around my age but looking a lot less tired and worn. His eyes were gentle and his face welcoming, with a long beard and warm smile. "Let's get you inside and find you some food, then you can tell me what brings you here."

I nodded, not really understanding his language, but by the time we entered the stones, we had gained some rudimentary form of communicating.

Inside the stones there were people of all ages—some were healers, others prepared food for the masses, some were hunters or gatherers returning with supplies. There were four priests, one for each direction. I saw cloth traders, some dealing in fur, some in silk and others in wool.

I was weak and unable to take everything in, and many came to my aid. I was taken to the priest in the south, who brought me food and a healer. The healer took one look at me and instantly knew what was wrong, and he spoke in words I could understand. I undid my wrap and showed him the bronze arrowheads and spearheads, and the gold trinkets, I explained if he helped me, I could teach others to make these things.

"This is a place of great power and health is restored to those who the Great Mother deems worthy, I can only hope that you are worthy. But pray tell me," he moved closer, and his voice dropped to a whisper, "which affliction is it you want cured? The leg, or the beast within?"

I hung my head, I was ashamed to tell him, but tell him I must.

"In all honesty, the leg. The wolf is strong, much stronger than I could ever be, and he is free. I have no wish to hurt anyone but I long for his power and the chance to run free from the limitations of this injured and aged body."

He nodded, handed me a bowl of food, and went to speak to the priest. I couldn't hear what they were saying and once my hunger was satiated, I curled up and slept in the warmth of the Henge. I dreamt of running through the woods and fields, along riverbanks and high into the mountains. So vivid was my dream, that I could smell the rich woody scents and the musk of the other animals that inhabited these lands. Eventually my healer returned, and I stirred on his approach.

"Well, my pilgrim, the Great Mother has approved your request, but all things have a price. The question is, is it a price you are willing to pay?"

"I can teach my craft, my gold and bronze weapons, and adornments are highly sought after—"

"—yes, yes, I know but while that is acceptable, there is still a higher price for your request."

"Name it!"

"I can heal your leg and you can change on the next full moon and run as wild and free as any wolf—no one shall hurt you, and you, in turn shall harm no one. In the morning, when the last star has left the dawn twilight sky, you shall once again be a man. More importantly, you will once again be a cripple, and you will spend the rest of your days teaching your craft. Such is the price you must pay."

"I know one night isn't much, but it's one night more than I have had in months, and just to experience that one night is something I would always be grateful for. So yes, this is a price I am willing to pay."

He nodded. "So be it." And with that he handed me a potion and a small stone with symbols carved into it. "Drink this and keep this trinket in you at all times."

"How? Where can I keep it as a wolf?"

"Lie down."

I did as instructed and I felt his hand close my eyes as if I were one of the dead. The next thing I remember is waking up with a pain in my jaw. I rubbed my face and saw him smiling at me.

"I have placed it in your gum where there was a missing tooth, it will come out upon your death."

The longest day came and went, and in the hazy summer days that followed, I upheld my end of the bargain and taught many young men and women my craft. I thought of my family often, but I knew I could never do more than wonder. I knew my mother had intended I find a cure for the 'beastly full moon curse' as she called it, and I also knew she would be disappointed if she knew the truth. How I longed for the full moon, even the agony of changing paled against the thrill of being a wolf. Ever since I had made my pact with the healer, it had consumed my every waking thought. The full moon couldn't come soon enough.

All day I felt restless, my entire body tingled at the thought of changing. I had worked harder than ever that day trying to ease my mind and quell my restlessness, but as the day began to fade, I found that I could contain myself no longer.

I filled my belly, this time more from habit than need, and headed out from the Henge and across the fields towards the hills and woodlands. The evening star lit up the dark cloudy skies of the dusk. Every inch of my body was tingling with anticipation. I had seen enough full moons to know this was never an easy metamorphosis, but I told himself that this time it would be worth the pain; everything would be different.

I stretched. There was a deep longing, an ache in my belly, and I was struggling to contain my ever-growing impatience. One night was all I had, and I desperately wished I had thought of asking for the longest night, but I suspected the Great Mother may have granted me nothing in exchange for my impudence. I tried hard to relax but found it impossible to do so. Resigned to having to wait for the moon to show her face I slumped down on a fallen tree trunk. That's when I felt the pins and needles tingling beneath my skin, and then came the searing pain, as my limbs cracked and lengthened. My heart pounded and my skin burned with savage ferocity as my body contorted and contracted. However painful the

44

metamorphosis, I savoured every agonising moment, and fortunately it was only moments.

As the pain subsided, I could hear my blood as it crashed through my veins like an ocean wave, and the fierce beat of my heart echoing throughout my body. I felt stronger than I ever had, my body was lean and powerful, and the night called to me. In this form, the darkness shared her mysteries. A preternatural orchestra accompanied the moonlight as it sang to me, and the taste of the sweet air filled my being. And oh, how the touch of the wind thrilled me as it gently kissed my fur in passing, and each scent excited my spirit. With every step, and every breath, I felt the Great Mother and her presence in all things, and I howled with gratitude for this precious gift.

I ran through fields and woods, I quenched my thirst from the river and satisfied my hunger with a hare. I had one night to be free, and I intended to indulge my animal instincts as much as possible. I had never hunted as a wolf, nor had I ever tasted raw flesh, but in that moment, it felt and tasted right.

As the moon began to set, I knew my freedom and strength were also coming to an end. I feebly howled a last thank you to the Great Mother—she had given me far more than I could ever have hoped for—before curling up on some soft grass and drifting off to sleep.

I was found the next morning by some villagers, about an hour or so from the Henge. I was naked, crippled, and beside me lay the small round talisman the priest had given me. It must have rolled out of my jaw when I changed back, although I have no memory of it.

In fact, I have no more memories at all.

FREEDOM—
WHERE'S THE WOLF?
Scott Irvine

Like the Talking Heads hit, *Once in a Lifetime*, I ask myself, well, how did I get here? There is no beautiful house or beautiful wife, only me, Nick White, standing alone before an abyss of constant thunder and lightning, driven by the dark chaos of the Great Serpent.

It is a realm beyond our normal existence; a kingdom of nothingness, yet it contains everything in the universe. It is transformation in a world where nothing changes, and I am preparing myself to enter into it. How can this be better than what I am running away from? Something that began on a small island off the Dorset coast, the Royal Manor of Portland.

On a wet and windy weekend in the spring, I was having a break with my partner, Sarah, staying at our friends Dave and Kim's house at the bottom of Wakeham. We were exploring the sculptures in Tout Quarry when the wind lashed off the Channel making even standing upright difficult. While I found shelter in an old quarry shed built into one of the stacks of old stone, the others dashed to the George Inn by the old church for a pint and maybe something to eat. I couldn't blame them, the weather was wild but according to the forecast, expected to blow over very quickly. The weather for the weekend was supposed to be sunny and warm, but not for the first time, it was totally wrong.

The eight-foot square and six-foot high room of stone blocks was an ideal place to watch the storm rage outside and enjoy a smoke in the dry. It was a shame about all the litter on the floor, putting me off sitting down. With nothing better to do, curiosity forced me to explore the gaps between the large stone blocks with the torch on my phone. In a gap by the doorway, something glistened in the light and I squeezed my fingers into it, through some sticky cobweb, to retrieve whatever it was, but something stung my index finger causing me to make a hasty retreat. I was in pain as I examined two puncture wounds on my fingertip.

"Bloody spiders!" I yelled, assuming it was a spider, trying to shake the pain away while grabbing a pen with my other hand to hook out the shiny object. It was a gold ring, a wedding band that had somehow found its way here, god knows when.

Then I heard what I thought was the howl of a wolf outside in the quarry, but obviously, there are no wolves on Portland. I assured myself it was just the wind. My finger began to hurt so much I began to feel faint and sat down on the dirty floor. For a short time, I watched ghostly figures come and go from the room; ancient workmen picking up and dropping off tools, and others, like myself, sheltering from a storm. I was drawn back to the present moment when I heard the howl again, louder this time, right outside the manmade cavern. A shadowy figure moved across the entrance, a man shape but animal in nature and I wished that I had joined the others in the pub.

By the time the pain had eased, the wind had become a breeze, the rain clouds had almost dispersed and the sun was trying to come out. I joined Sarah and our friends in the pub; they all thought my experience hilarious, and the ring a cheap 9 carat worth about £60 at best.

That evening we celebrated a full moon ritual with friends of Dave and Kim, Clan Dolmen, at the Circle of Stones in Tout Quarry, and returned home to Helland on Bodmin Moor the following morning.

I thought nothing of the bite until almost a month later, on the eve of the next full moon. Sarah was at work on nightshift at Bodmin Hospital and I was pottering around the cottage, bored, and came across the ring that I had stashed in a bits and bobs dish when I got back from Portland. Without thinking, I put it on and immediately, I heard the howl of a wolf somewhere on the Moor. I went outside to see if anything was there. The moon was rising above the treeline over Blissland to the east, and I suddenly felt at peace with nature and no longer bored, just an urge to run towards the moon and into the woods from whence the howling came.

Again, without thinking, I joined the howling pack of wolves, my family, working up a frenzy of excitement as to what the power of Luna would bring this wonderful evening. Once we had settled down, we made our way to Helland's sister village, Blissland, ignoring several villagers taking an evening stroll along the country lanes, visiting friends, not stopping for anything until we reached a small cottage on the outskirts. In the garden was a middle-aged man sitting by a fire, drinking beer and before I knew it, the pack leapt on him, ripping him apart in a bloody frenzy. I could not help but join in and enjoy the bliss of teeth tearing into flesh and bone, and the smell of fear. I loved the smell of fear probably above anything else.

Licking our lips, we moved northwards towards St. Breward and another sacrifice to the Gods. This time it was a woman, who unfortunately for her, had left her lounge window open. Her dog quickly stopped barking and gave us no trouble as we poured through the window and went for her throat. I felt the same bloodlust as before and the fear was strong, causing me to be one of the first to attack, ripping out the woman's throat and tasting her fresh pumping blood as it flowed into my belly. I felt alive, nature was alive, and the world was alive. I was wild, and importantly, I was free to be myself.

Sated, we left the cottage and followed the Camel River out of the village and back towards home, washing ourselves in the fast flowing stream and frolicking on the banks. I was free and feeling lustful. I climbed onto the back of a she-wolf, or Fae, only to feel a powerful nip on my neck from the Alpha. She was his and I was out of order. Hey, it was my first night as a wolf, how was I to know? The moon was high in the heavens when I reached home and crawled into a ball on the floor in our lounge.

"What the hell are you doing on the floor, Nick?" Sarah yelled at me when she got home in the early hours. "You been at that weed again! You said you would stop," she barked, taking off her coat and putting the kettle on. The coffee stirred me awake.

"That was a weird dream," I muttered. "I was a wolf, hunting people in Blissland and St. Breward." My mouth tasted foul, my stomach ached and my neck hurt.

"Have you been bitten by a dog?" Sarah queried, pulling back my shirt collar. "It looks like a dog bite. What did you get up to last night?"

All I remembered of last night was the dream; a very vivid dream that I could still remember all the details of—the smells, and the emotions—even now.

"I must have caught my neck on something," I told her. "It's just a funny looking bruise."

"Well it looks like a dog bite, whatever it is," Sarah announced before reminding me I would be late for work if I didn't get a move on.

That evening we heard of the savage murders in Blissland and St. Breward; the bodies of a man and a women were discovered that morning, ripped limb from limb, the flesh torn from the bones and chewed on. The connection to the pair, according to the police, was they were both private landlords of many local properties around the Bodmin area. Sarah knew better; gossip travels fast, especially where Sarah works. Jack Brown and Debby Summers were having an affair, something that had been going on for nearly a year, according to Carol, Sarah's best friend, who was very good at knowing everyone else's business. Their affair was really no secret in the villages but in their minds, it could not have been murder because they knew no one who would commit such a heinous act in such a beautiful area of Cornwall.

"Sounds like your dream," Sarah said, to which I shrugged my shoulders and reaffirmed it was just a dream.

But secretly, I was not so sure now. It felt real—the disgusting taste in my mouth when

53

I'd woken and the bite mark on my neck were real. I convinced myself it was the work of the ring, in a Lord of the Rings kind of way. The ring had transformed me into a kind of skin walker, a werewolf, but things like that did not exist.

I must have replaced the ring in the bits and bobs dish when I returned last night because I did not have it on this morning, and here it was, back in its place. The following morning I put the ring in an old tobacco pouch and buried it in the garden next to the lupins.

I was hoping Sarah would stay at home with me on the next full moon, just in case, but she had to go to Carol's hen party in Bodmin. The best thing for me, I decided, was a sleeping pill and an early night.

I had another vivid dream, meeting up with the pack in the woods, tearing apart a man in Washaway, westwards across the river. This time it all went wrong, we were ambushed by hunters who shot one of us dead and wounded two others. I had part of my ear shot off and have never been so scared in my life. I woke up on the lounge floor again, the tip of my ear bloody and painful. My mouth tasted disgusting and my stomach churned like molten lava. It had been real.

"We need to talk," Sarah instructed as she handed me a coffee. "I thought you buried the ring. It is still lying on the top of the bits and bobs dish."

"I did bury it," I argued. "I have no idea how it got back there."

When Sarah had returned from the hen night around one in the morning, I had been nowhere to be seen. She'd heard me return at 3.32am, stumble about downstairs for a bit, curl up on the floor and go to sleep.

"A man has been killed," she shrieked, "and I think you have something to do with it." Sarah, put her arms around me and gave me a hug. "We need to do something about it."

"I agree," I responded. "And before the next full moon."

News quickly spread around the villages of another gruesome attack, an elderly retired priest was attacked, and this time, one of the murderers had been shot dead and another two men were under police guard in Plymouth Hospital. The hunters who killed a man running away from the scene were sure they were firing on a pack of wild dogs, not humans, but it was dark despite a full moon. They were as shocked as anyone was, finding a dead man. A nurse had phoned the police when two men arrived at the hospital with bullet wounds, one serious. The police were sure they had the whole gang of psychopaths involved in the recent killings—case solved.

After contacting Dave and Kim on Portland, we were pretty much ordered to return the ring and join them for a ceremony with the local witches at the next full moon. We met at the Circle of Stones at dusk, witnessing our star sink below the sea before gathering around the roach stone altar as the moon rose over the workshop roofs of the nearby industrial site. Midway through the ceremony, the high priestess marked out a symbol on my forehead that caused me to phase out and arrive at the edge of the abyss. I could hear the whisper of the high priestess in my mind, "Move into the abyss."

"What then?" I questioned.

For a while, the high priestess said nothing, then, "Your curse could be lifted, or you could die. Everything could stay the same or you could remain a wolf for the rest of your life. You might enter another dimension, an alternative reality or be reborn as a newborn baby, possibly with all the knowledge you possess now or more than likely, no knowledge at all. Quite simply, you might become crazy, insane and need to be locked away, or you might wake up at a time before your holiday on Portland. What happens to you is up to the Gods, I hope you have been honouring a good God or Goddess."

I held my breath and stepped into the abyss to accept my fate, wishing I had a God or Goddess that I knew.

DATE NIGHT
Kevin Groves

Toby was anxious. First dates always made him nervous. This one in particular was set up through a very select dating website recommended by a vague friend he had known for what felt like centuries.

Or perhaps his nervousness was due to the fact that it was cold, dark and overcast, with the rain running down his neck, while waiting outside in the park for his date.

In his mind he weighed up if this was a great move or not. Eventually he concluded that they should have met at the restaurant. Why didn't they? Ah yes, she wanted to meet outside first. Nice.

The park was empty of people and the bushes were dark and swaying, as if a rampaging army of cats were having it out with one another.

Then he saw her. In fact he heard her first, her high heels clicking on the path. This had to be her, no one else in this awful weather would choose to be here right now.

Elizabeth, or Beth as she preferred, was wrapped in a dark coat. Her hands tucked into her pockets, collar turned up and a beanie hat on top and only her shins poking out from under the bottom of her coat.

Once she was close enough he could make out her face, he gasped at her beauty. Even on such a night like this, her make-up was perfect.

She held out her arms and they embraced. Heavenly it was; her scent intoxicating. With both smiling, they linked arm-in-arm and left the park to go to the restaurant over the road.

On entering, their coats were taken and he forgot himself completely and let out a whistle, which he quickly felt foolish and embarrassed about.

She was absolutely stunning; her off the shoulder red dress, long blonde hair, and thin red scarf around her neck, gave her a 1940's French look. Classy. He realised he'd been looking at her for too long, and the waiter was waiting for him to follow.

"You look great!" He blurted out to cover himself. "You look good enough to eat!" He felt his blush and flustered. Not going very well at all. He hoped she wasn't having second thoughts about this crazy guy. She reassured him with a touch on his arm, and smiled as if reading his thoughts.

"All in good time." She softly laughed with a twinkle in her eyes and led him along behind the waiter. His panic subsided with great relief.

The hours flew by as if a dream. They talked, ate, drank and talked. All night, until they were the last in the restaurant. The food

59

and company, he decided, was perfection and she seemed to have enjoyed herself too. Such a great idea coming to this place—his favourite restaurant—as they prepare his rare stake exactly to his taste.

Back out into the cold and separate taxis for both of them. He wasn't going to push his luck on the first date, and to be honest with all the anxiety, he really didn't think it would be wise.

They promised to go on a second date.

A day or so of continued anxiety and she called him. He was blown away. She suggested a day out.

A couple of weeks of regular dates, including a couple of quick kisses, which were nice. He felt so good, which was great, in fact. It was good to be in love once again.

And to be honest they were getting on so well it was like they had known each other all their lives. Nothing he could think of was annoying and he hoped it was mutual. Well, there was one thing, one tiny little thing which he noticed. Every time they were together, whatever she wore, she always had a small scarf around her neck. It was nothing really, and it always suited her. Nothing to pick holes in really.

His nerves were particularly raised once again. The relationship was moving along and after last night's snogging session at the back of the cinema, like teenagers they weren't, they seemed to have naturally become more comfortable with one another and were ready to wordlessly move on to the more physical side of their relationship.. He wanted this to work. Their mutual feelings of desire, he knew, were driving them both of late.

He hadn't felt this nervous in years. So strange. Was this the one perhaps? She was very special.

Another date night and it was likely this one would be the acid test, and a significant one he thought. Beth wanted to cook at her home. That was a clear signal right? Code for something? Oh boy. His stomach churned with anxiety.

He stood on the doorstep in the brilliant moonlight as she answered the door. Her minimalist home was perfect, much like every other aspect of her he had come to love. Tonight was no different, as far as getting dressed up, which surprised him; they were staying in right? But again he noticed the scarf. A small blue one that matched her slinky blue dress. His blood boiled and he felt he would melt right there.

Telling himself to calm down and actually talk would be a good move. Though her smile made it clear she knew exactly what he was thinking.

Dinner was nice and light—he admired the token thought because they both knew what tonight was really about. Afterwards they slumped down on the sofa with drinks.

To his surprise, Beth suggested they watch a scary movie while their dinner went down. Not his thing, but he soon understood the real reasons as they could snuggle up nice and tight and hold on to each other during the scary bits. Again he admired her planning. Fantastic idea.

They clung to one another. Hands going places.

His heart thumped in his chest, louder than it had ever done before. His blood burned through his body. He yearned for more. Eventually his lips touched her shoulder and moved along towards her neck. Lost in the moment, his lips followed her collar bone and the base of her neck—then a mouthful of scarf.

Before Beth could object, he moved a hand from her breast and tugged at the scarf. Suddenly his lips were no longer in contact with skin. He opened his eyes. Her head wasn't there.

"Down here," Beth whispered. He looked into her lap and saw her head staring back up at him. "Would you kindly reattach my head please? Until I can find some new bolts I am relying on that scarf to keep my head in place."

"Of... course..." His shock leaving his mouth flapping. Then, quite calmly, as if this was perfectly normal, he lifted the head and placed it back on her shoulders. Beth fumbled with the scarf and watched him.

"Are you OK?" she asked, as if nothing unusual had just happened. He was sitting back on the sofa, his face flushed and sweaty.

"I'm OK, and to tell the truth I wasn't expecting that."

"You don't look OK. I was going to tell you eventually," she replied.

"Well if we have secrets then I should share mine." Toby was sweating profusely now. This was not turning out to be the night he'd expected. He began to shake violently. His body ripped and his face began to elongate, and teeth enlarge.

"Oh great!" Beth exclaimed. "A werewolf! I've never dated a werewolf before! What a great match the monster dating website did. I love a guy who's wild in bed. Come on!" She grabbed him and dragged him off to the bedroom.

WARD 9 – THE ZOO
Diane Narraway

"I suspect you're wondering why I asked you here, Dr Lovelace, or may I call you Henry?"

"Yes of course, and yes, I was rather."

"Well, you see, I have a matter of some delicacy I wish to discuss with you ... I have a patient, a young woman by the name of Mara, whose surname is unknown, on ward nine ..."

"... Ward nine! I mean, isn't that ... well, isn't that the zoo?"

"I believe, some call it that, yes."

"I'm not sure how I can help. I am, of course, very flattered by your invitation, Dr Phelps, that you requested I visit, but your expertise is far beyond mine. I am merely a junior physician."

"Ah well, that's the thing, I am not after a medical or psychiatric second opinion, I am more interested in your knowledge of folklore."

"Folklore! It's just a hobby, I am no expert, but I will help if I can."

"Let me explain. I need to tell you her story, such as we have managed to ascertain.

She was brought in to us several months ago. The young woman in question had been found one midsummer morning stark naked in the wolf enclosure of the local zoo. When she arrived, myself and the nurse on duty carried

65

out a thorough examination. There was no sign of any sexual or physical assault, yet nor was there any sign of her clothes.

This was followed by a psychiatric assessment, during which she informed me that she changes once a month, when the moon is full, into a wolf."

"Lycanthropy?"

"Lycanthropy yes, and although that in itself is not uncommon, this is an exceptional case. She claims she has done this since puberty, and says it is something that she has no control over. Naturally, I felt the need to keep her here in order to observe her actions during the following full moon. I have to tell you, Henry, I am glad I did as this has proved to be an exceptional case. So far, she has baffled not only myself, but also the select few other esteemed physicians I have shared this with."

"How so?"

"Well, that's why I invited you here tonight. That is, on this particular night, as it is a full moon. I would like you to observe her behaviour. I would very much like to hear your thoughts on the matter. Follow me, and don't worry, you are perfectly safe. Although I must warn you she has cost me a nurse. Unfortunately, Nurse Roberts, the nurse on duty when the young woman was brought in, was unable to cope with Mara's full moon activities and ended up becoming a patient herself.

Fortunately, Nurse Williams arrived a couple of months ago and from day one she has been a godsend. I don't mind telling you, I'd be lost without her. Only a few weeks into the job she saw Mara's monthly behaviour and coped admirably. She is the height of discretion, and as such, is the only nurse allowed on that ward"

"Good evening Dr Phelps, I see you have brought another along to visit me this time. I reckon I must be your most intriguing patient, or are you going to be charging folks to see me soon? Am I merely destined to be a freak in your cabinet of human curiosities?"

"Settle down Mara, I have just brought along Dr Lovelace here, for his opinion on your condition, and as always, I have brought Nurse Williams with me. You are my patient, and as such I will do whatever I can to ease your suffering.

In case you're wondering, Henry, which I am sure you are, I always have Nurse Williams present as a precautionary measure. Mara can get quite agitated and well, you'll see, I just feel there are times when us men and our sensibilities need a chaperone!"

"I see, Dr Phelps."

"I doubt you do my good man, but you will most certainly understand by the end of the night. I would not dare leave any man alone with her. It's starting, look! Quick cover your ears"

"Good Lord, does she always howl like that? Thank God, you warned me, otherwise I feel sure my eardrums would have burst. And oh my! How does she contort like that? Are her limbs growing longer? How is that even possible?"

"I believe she is somehow dislocating them, so they appear to grow. More curious is how she can still move about on them. No! No! Don't get too close to the bars, my good man, you could get hurt when she starts thrashing about. Her nails, or rather her claws, can be quite long and extremely painful. I got too close once and have the scars to show for it."

"Is it possible that this is part of her menstrual cycle? Women tend not to possess all their faculties around that time, and although I can see she is still quite young, perhaps she is reaching an early menopause?"

"Of course, we considered this but there is no correlation between this and her monthly courses. In fact, by comparison to some, she is most agreeable at that time. However, nothing can be ruled out."

"I can honestly say I have never seen anything like this. The way she writhes and twists, it's as if she is actually turning into a wolf, which of course is not in the slightest bit possible. I have only seen but a few cases of those suffering from the delusion of Lycanthropy. In all instances, they have been prone to weak howling, pacing back and forth, and scratching at the door. In every case there has been no physical change. Certainly, there is no dislocation of the limbs. Ah, now I see her claws. How is that possible? Surely one cannot dislocate one's nails to lengthen them.

My word does she always rip at her clothes so frantically?"

"I cannot explain her claws, I am at a loss regarding that. As for her clothes being torn off, so far, yes, which is why I insist on a chaperone. You see, Henry, within the first 10-15 minutes, all her clothes are removed and even in this grotesque form, she still has very feminine features. You see, now, why I insist on Nurse Williams' presence."

"Indeed, I do, she is quite a marvel! And her actions are, by her nature, animalistic and more erotic than any sideshow stripper. It is a credit to you Sir, that you seek to alleviate her suffering, many would not be so honourable.

I will do some digging and see if I can shed any light on her condition, but I'm not sure I hold out much hope. However, Dr Phelps, I am eternally grateful for the opportunity to have witnessed something so unique. Pray tell me, what is she like the rest of the month?"

"The rest of the month she is charming, I would even venture to say quite lovely. Were I in the market for a wife, I may well consider her for such, but not with such an affliction. Let us retire, as morning approaches and she will soon be asleep. Such is her pattern."

"Nurse Williams, is that you?"

"Yes Mara, they've gone, and I've brought you a blanket, some fresh clothes and some food. Are you alright? You haven't hurt yourself, have you?"

"No, I'm fine, I just need some food and sleep. You are so very kind Nurse Williams."

"Well, someone has to look after you, don't they? Those doctors certainly don't. I had to wait until Dr Phelps left for the city. He so rarely leaves this place, but I believe he will be away for a few days on business, so how about I sneak you out for some fresh air? There's a circus in town, we could go there if you like."

"Oh, that would be wonderful!"

"I'll fetch you a hat and coat, I keep a spare in the cloak room. We'll sneak out, the others won't notice. It's only me and Dr Phelps who come down here, everyone else thinks this ward is just a myth. They call it the Zoo, a mythical ward that houses those who are considered abominations, not fit for fairs and circuses."

"And yet, here I am amongst them. How I hate it here, scratching around in this stinking cell, half-starved, and for what? As entertainment for Dr Phelps and whichever associate he brings to watch. I swear I am just erotic fuel for his perverse fantasies. If I'm destined to be a freak, I would rather join the circus and be paid for it, than sit here in in filth and squalor."

"I know this place, I've been here before. I know you too don't I ... Mother?"

"Oh Mara, I could kiss you. And now look, you've made me cry. Where did I put that hanky? I can never find anything in these confounded nurses' skirts. I have waited months to hear you call me that again."

"I have a daughter too, don't I? And am I a trapeze artist? It's all coming back to me now. But how did I end up in the wolf enclosure of the local zoo? I can't remember anything about that day, other than being taken to the sanatorium. Do you know what happened?"

"You fell off the trapeze, trying new routine. Somehow you missed the safety net and you hit the floor. We thought you were going to die. It was a full moon that night, and we hoped that if you changed it might make you strong enough to survive. It did, but at what cost? You were unconscious and we assumed

... Honestly? I don't know what we assumed, but we would never have put you through any of that intentionally. Oh, now look, more tears. For the love of the goddess, will I ever find that hanky?"

"Don't cry. I've done plenty for all of us, and at least you didn't put me on display that night... Talking of which, I have a hazy memory of being a freak here, but surely that can only happen once a month. Can't it? And do I, you know, completely change? Do I actually become a wolf?"

"You do, and a very beautiful wolf at that. The only reason you didn't fully change in that awful excuse for a sanitorium is because you were hidden away in the basement. You were deprived of the light of the moon, and more importantly, you were hidden away from the light of the goddess. Bloody charlatans, calling themselves doctors. Clueless idiots, the lot of them!

The women of our family have always been blessed by the goddess. As children, they change on the waxing crescent moon, at puberty the waxing half-moon, at childbearing age the full moon. In the few years leading up to the menopause it is the waning half-moon, and at menopause the waning crescent moon. Of course, those of us older ladies who have left our childbearing years behind, we change on the dark moon. So you see, for 7 nights a month there is nearly always a freak on display."

"What happens the rest of the time?"

"The rest of the time we are a traditional circus, with some exceptional performers and fortune tellers."

"And I'm not sure if I'm remembering or just guessing, but I don't think your surname is really Williams either—is it?"

"No, it most certainly is not! It is the same as yours, Mara Lupez, and you my love, are not the favourite erotic freak in Dr Phelps' menagerie of abominations. You are my daughter, the incredible, the wondrous and beautiful flying Mara. You are the star performer and extremely talented trapezist in the most prestigious Lucan Thorpe's travelling circus."

"And I'm home!"

THE WOMAN UPSTAIRS
Jennie Jones

Bleep ... Bleep ... So much bleeping in the world these days.

The supermarket checkout rings out like birds singing. The bleeps are high-pitched and determined. Sometimes rhythmic. Always hypnotic. And oddly comforting. Without the bleeps, the supermarket would be too quiet—so many people, stood so close together in line, and all so deadly quiet. It would be horrible.

I join the checkout queue, and peer into the other shoppers' baskets. What are they buying? Family food? Party food? Diet food? One's groceries can say a lot about someone.

There's a young woman in front of me. She's buying a tonne of meat—packs of cut-price steak, liver, and even a tray of tripe. No vegetables. No fruit. Just lots of meat, and a bottle of red wine.

She wears tight jeans and a green Parka coat with the hood up. Why does she have so much meat? As she looks up to pay, I catch sight of her face. She's one of my neighbours from the complex around the corner, though we have yet to introduce ourselves.

She hunts in her pocket for small change. She is 30p short. I dig out the coins from my purse, and reach forwards.

"Here."

"Oh … thanks."

The bill paid, she shuffles forwards. She waits for me by the door, and we walk out of the shop together, and into the busy street. It's 5pm. We push through the throng of shoppers and commuters, both keen to reach our respective flats, just a couple of minutes' walk away.

"Planning a barbecue?" I ask, which is ridiculous as it is November. And although we're lucky to have a communal garden, we don't have any barbecue facilities.

But the woman doesn't smile. She doesn't even acknowledge what I suppose was a stupid comment. We walk for a few moments in silence. Then she speaks. She says her name is Aimee.

"Doreen," I reply. "You live upstairs from me?"

"Yes."

She says she's been up there six weeks. No partner. No pets or children. She lives alone.

We reach our front door, and step inside the porch. On the wall is a noticeboard with a missing cat poster. There have been a few missing cats lately.

"What job do you do?" I ask.

"Sales. On my laptop. I work from home."

76

"Oh ... That sounds interesting."

She shrugs.

"Well, bye," she says. And she's gone. I don't get chance to ask more.

But I'm curious. I want to know more. Some might call me nosy, but I like to think I'm a caring neighbour. I suppose she must have been stocking up her freezer, to have bought so much meat. What other explanation could there be?

I don't see Aimee again for a few weeks. But I know she's up there. I hear her footsteps on the boards. But no other noise. No TV. No loud music. She should be the perfect neighbour, but I'm uneasy. I sense there is something amiss.

The next time I see her is in the hallway by the letter boxes. She jumps, startled, as I approach.

"You look dreadful," I say.

Her face is so hairy - there is a soft, downy, but dark fuzz across her cheeks and forehead. She also has dark shadows under her eyes. She pulls her hood up, and flips her sunglasses down.

"Sorry, I didn't mean to be rude," I say.

But she starts to cry. I'm such a clot—I'm always making people cry. I should be more tactful. I put my hand on her shoulder, to console her.

"Are you sure you're OK?"

"Yeah, yeah," she says. "I'm just a bit tired, that's all. Too many late nights."

"Really? Are you sure that's all it is?"

"And a bit of iron deficiency," she adds. "But I'm working on that."

"What, after all that meat you eat?"

"I guess so."

"Have you seen a doctor?"

I can see her eyes through her sunglasses, staring at me.

"With all due respect, how is this any of your business?"

And that is the end of the conversation. She grabs her mail, and tiptoes back upstairs without another word.

I also return to my flat. I sink into my armchair, feeling terrible. Had I been intrusive? Maybe. It wouldn't be the first time I'd been told to back off. But, as always, I'd only wanted to help.

One thing's for sure though—she's ill. She's an injured and distressed animal. She needs looking after. She's lucky I'm here, and that I'm tough-skinned.

When I'm at the pharmacy later that day, I buy a tub of iron tablets. I rush back and knock on her door. There's no answer, but I know she's in there. No matter—I leave the tub by her door. She'll find them if and when she comes out.

But as the evening arrives, I become more concerned. I can't hear any footsteps on my ceiling. She's too quiet.

What if she's seriously ill? What if she's collapsed and is unconscious? She really did look unwell earlier. She's all alone up there. I haven't heard any visitors drop by.

What to do?

I decide that I'll pop upstairs in the morning, and see how she is. So I lock up, brush my teeth, climb into bed, and try to put her out of my mind.

I eventually fall asleep, but I don't get as far as morning. Sometime in the early hours, I'm woken by the sound of rustling outside my bedroom window. My flat is on the ground floor, and backs on to the lawn and shrubbery.

I lie there, in the dark, listening intently. But all I can now hear is the sound of my heart thumping.

Could it be a burglar? If it is, he—or she—will find a way into the building. There's no point hiding from this. And besides, I'm the Neighbourhood Watch co-ordinator. I need to deal with this.

I climb out of bed, and pull on a dressing gown before creeping over to the window. I open it an inch, ready to slam it shut if needed.

"Hello," I call. "Is anyone there?"

It's all quiet, and I feel silly. It was probably an animal—maybe a cat, or a fox, or even a hedgehog. But then I make out the outline of a person, stood in the middle of the lawn.

"Aimee? Is that you?"

She's dressed in her pyjamas, and is cradling a cat in her arms.

My eyes adjust under the full moon, and I look more closely. The cat is bleeding. There is a deep gash on its neck, though it's still alive, and whimpering. Aimee has blood around her mouth, and blood on her clothes.

"What's going on? What have you done to the cat?"

And then she is gone, into the night. I shut the window, checking it is locked. And then check my front door is locked. And then I turn my computer on.

Where to start? I need information on this.

Hypertrichosis pops up on my Google search. This is the medical term for an abnormal amount of hair in the wrong places. In days gone by, sufferers used to be found in circus freak shows. But these days, the condition is rare. There are fewer than 50 cases documented worldwide. But this doesn't explain the eating of live animals. I can't find anything about that, except under mental illness and delusions.

The next morning, I go upstairs and knock on her door.

"You have to stop eating cats," I shout through the wood, when she doesn't answer.

The door opens. I step inside.

"Why cats? Why not a pig, or a sheep?"

"Why not? Why is one animal fair game, and the other banished from our menus?" she replies.

"But they're people's pets? Don't you feel guilty?"

"A little. But I need raw meat. I can't survive without it."

"Really?"

She certainly looks better this morning. Normal, in fact. The excess hair is gone, and her skin is soft and glowing. The tiredness also appears to have lifted.

"Don't worry. I don't eat humans," she says.

"I think you have some explaining to do," I say. I try to sound authoritative, but my words sound shaky. This wasn't what I was expecting.

I go through to her kitchen, and put the kettle on. And then bring through two mugs of tea into the living room. There's only one chair—a fold-up camping chair, positioned at a fold-up camping table. She moves to let me have the chair, and sits cross-legged on a cushion on the floor.

"I don't have much furniture," she says. "I move around a lot."

She tells me she had a happy childhood, but the condition developed—almost overnight—in her late teens. At which point, her horrified parents tried to have her

81

committed. She ran away... and that, she says, is pretty much it.

"So, where do we go from here?" I ask.

She shrugs.

"I don't think the police would believe you," she says. "And besides, I disposed of the evidence."

"What, all of it?" I asked.

"Nothing goes to waste," she says. "I don't like it, but hey ho—we can't always control what life throws at us."

But there has to a be solution, I say. Some kind of work-around. She reckons she's tried everything, from eating raw meat from the butcher, to vitamin supplements, and even hypnosis. But nothing works.

"Raw meat isn't enough on its own," she says. "It needs to be fresh meat, if you get my meaning... still with a pulse, with its eyes open."

"That's horrible," I say.

"Just the way it is," she says. "I don't have a choice."

But I'm not convinced. She can't have tried everything. Every problem has a solution. She just has to find it.

"I'll help you," I offer. But she isn't convinced.

But as luck would have it, I find the solution later that day. Sometimes it just takes a fresh pair of eyes to spot it.

WOLF IT DOWN dog food—a dry food alternative to raw meat. Supposedly it contains all the essential ingredients of raw meat, but in a 'convenient, hygienic pellet' form.

When I get home, I take it straight up to her.

She looks suspiciously at it.

"Dog food?"

"Try it," I urge.

"But it's not fresh. Not alive."

She picks out a pellet, and pops it in her mouth.

"Mmm, OK, I suppose."

She takes a handful, and munches down on them.

"Some dogs prefer it," I say. "Or so said the man in the pet shop."

"The pet shop? You shouldn't believe everything you're told," replies Aimee. "But it has potential. I'll see how I get on with it."

Not long after that, she moves out. I didn't even realise she was going, until I came home to find a bunch of flowers and a card propped up against my door.

There was a message in the card: "I love my new food, x", and 30p sellotaped inside. I put the card and flowers on my mantelpiece. Another successful project ticked off.

Later that day, I head back out to the supermarket to get some groceries. As I stand in line, listening to the check-out bleeps, I remember my first encounter with Aimee. As I

gaze into the baskets ahead of me, I wonder
who my new neighbour will be.

FROM HUNTER TO WOLF
Gary Hawker

HUNTER'S MOON

When a homeless man was found dead on the common, nobody was that perturbed. The loose group he was associated with were renowned for their drunken brawls. His throat had been ripped open and, with no other obvious explanations, this was put down to the violent application of the jagged edge of a broken bottle. Despite the best efforts of the police, nobody was arrested.

Exactly four weeks later, a full moon again passing uninterrupted through the October night sky, a couple were attacked about a mile away from the original incident. Their bodies had been savaged as if by a pack of dogs. No such pack was identified and the nature of the injuries remained a mystery. The papers made the most of it, highlighting amongst other things, the fact that the yellow dress the woman had been wearing was missing as well as a locket she'd worn around her neck.

Frank feared for his two daughters, Maisie and Sue. With Karen, his wife, they made sure that they were never on their own. They had only just been trusted with walking from the school back home, but now one or other of the parents insisted that they picked them up. Other families reacted in a similar manner. An unspoken panic spread across the community like a contagion.

A week or so later, Frank was digging over his allotment when he spotted something bright and yellow stuffed under a flowerpot. He called the police immediately and the area was cordoned off as a potential crime scene. The dress was indeed the one worn by the murdered woman, but unfortunately any fingerprints or other forensic evidence remained inconclusive. This finding did nothing to placate everyone's fears, the panic maturing into full-blown terror. People restricted visits to the town's open spaces with some parents forbidding their children to leave the house. Needless to say, everyone was dreading the next full moon.

BEAVER MOON

The air smelt of bonfires and spent fireworks, the moon elusive behind the low clouds, occasionally peeping through like a child trying to see what was going on in the world. Families remained tentative and watchful of their children but the celebrations trumped their fears and everyone ambled to the beach to witness the firework display launched from boats anchored in the bay. The council provided safe areas, an additional platoon of volunteers and a lost child point, highlighted by a huge neon arrow pointing downward.

Frank and Karen marched their girls around in tight formation, making sure they were always within touching distance. Frank knew he may have been a little too zealous but, as every parent is aware, paranoia comes with the job. What was unsettling was that no suspects had been identified let alone arrests being made. They were a small seaside community and nothing had ever happened like this in living memory.

When the last firework bloomed, lighting up both sky and sea, one loose spark fell over the face of the moon like a golden tear. The crowd let out a collective sigh of appreciation and a group of youths let out a series of whoops and cheers. Everything was as it should be as the families turned their backs on the beach and made their way home.

Frank was relieved when he shut the front door and ushered the children to their beds. It was late. There would be no stories tonight, it was school the next day. The house quiet, Frank and Karen uncorked a bottle of wine and filled the silence with the mundane reassuring chitchat favoured by couples who had been together for some time.

Nearing the end of the bottle, Frank heard, or thought he heard, a shuffling of their bins. He downed his wine in one gulp and insisted that he checked it out. Karen thought it was foxes but allowed her husband his assumed right of portraying himself as the family's protector. Although she knew what he was thinking, she told him not to worry and announced she was going to bed.

Outside, the street was still and silent, nobody was about. The bins were where they should be, the garden gate was bolted and all was in order, but as he turned, a passing shadow caught in his peripheral vision. A myriad of scenarios immediately crowded his head. After a moment of hesitation, he decided to follow his instincts and pursue this shadow, whatever it was. Twenty minutes later, he found himself back on the esplanade, the bonfire had lost its flames but embers were swirling around in the breeze like restless glowworms. A few workers were attending to it, just to make sure it stayed within its confines. Frank told himself off for being so obsessive and made his way home again.

The following morning, the family awoke to the news that one of the volunteers had been found on the beach, her face bloody and disfigured. The wounds were so horrific that, at first, nobody could identify her. She had been breathing when they lifted her into the ambulance, but died on her way to the hospital. It wasn't until her partner contacted the police to report her missing that they put two and two together.

As all three incidents had happened when the moon was full, the papers began talking about the Werewolf Murders. This naturally caught the attention of the world beyond but did little to comfort the inhabitants of the sleepy town.

COLD MOON

It was almost as if, Frank reckoned to his wife, the nation was waiting for the full moon with as much excitement as anticipation. It was almost as if, he continued, they would be disappointed if someone wasn't butchered like the last poor souls.

The town felt it was under martial law. Everyone was on their guard. Police officers, usually invisible, were walking amongst them in weaponised gangs. On the day of the cold moon, cars were being stopped, the homes of past miscreants were raided at dawn. Police officers boarded trains and buses. The overall purpose was to prevent the same thing happening again and to reassure the citizens that the authorities were on the case. On both accounts they failed. People doubted whether the murder or murders could actually be prevented—all agreed this was a slick and brutal professional at work—and as far as reassurance was concerned, the sheer number of officers seemed to do the exact opposite.

Of course, for every officer of the law there was a journalist. Considering four innocent people had been murdered, they had the collective demeanour of people waiting for the visit of a celebrity. When interviewing locals, only a few of them seemed sincere, the rest struggled to hide their delight.

Frank and Karen decided to keep their children home with them. Despite ignoring the official guidance, they weren't the only ones to do this. Laws could be broken or disregarded if it conflicted with the need to shield your loved ones. The weather was bitterly cold; there had been heavy frosts for a week now. There had been innumerable snowfalls with many arriving late at work because of accidents or the fact that it took a good half an hour to scrape the ice from the windscreens.

Frank had tried to keep the heating low but with all the family protesting that they could hardly see each other behind their ghostly breath, he relented and turned the heating up a couple of notches. I suppose, he thought to himself, the important thing in this crazy time was to keep everyone as happy as possible.

The Cold Moon fell on his friend Jake's birthday and, despite his protest, there was to be a birthday gathering in his local pub. In the end, the birthday boy picked up that other parents were equally anxious and rearranged it as a late afternoon/early evening event. Every father, he announced magnanimously, will be home by nine pm. Frank told his wife that this should be fine, as all murders happened either near midnight or not long afterwards. Anyway, there were police patrolling up and down the streets throughout the night.

On the day, knowing there would be an effective curfew, every one of his mates drank as quickly as possible and most were very drunk by eight. Some gave in to their vice and stayed but not Frank; he staggered home, taking a well-lit short cut along the back water. At one point, he sat on a bench and instantly fell asleep, but something deep within him woke him up and he became immediately aware of his precarious situation. He pulled himself up and stumbled onward.

In the morning, he was awoken by a scream from his wife.

"What's happened to you?" she yelled.

"Nothing's happened to me!"

"Well," she said, putting her hand to her mouth, "look in the mirror."

He, too, let out a muffled yelp when he saw that his clothes were dishevelled, torn in places, covered in dirt, with pools of dried blood covering the left side of his face from his nose and into his hair. He stripped his clothes off, noticing a few bruises over his torso, and got into the shower. It was only after he had returned to normal that he confessed to his wife that he had been steaming-drunk and must

92

have fallen and hit his face. She accepted his explanation but added that Jake, in her opinion, had always been a bad influence.

They put off watching the news, afraid that there had been yet another murder—while they didn't know, it really hadn't happened. It remained that way until a neighbour called in to tell them the news that two journalists, a male and female, had been found 'torn to pieces' down by the harbour.

"Bloody hell," Frank gasped, "I was down that way last night!"

As soon as Karen said the words 'lucky escape', she turned abruptly to her husband, thinking of the state he was in that morning. He could read her thoughts: luckier than anyone would know.

WOLF MOON

Christmas came and went that year. The celebrations were somewhat muted and most either stayed at home or flew off to holiday destinations south of Valencia. Frank and Karen made the most of it, placating their children's fears while suppressing their own. The police presence was stepped up and became normalised in the town. Several clues were followed up and they made positive announcements that they were very close to making a breakthrough. They had blood from the perpetrator and were embarking on a methodical house-to-house DNA sampling, whilst eliminating the obvious from their enquiries. Frank and his wife would be tested but not the children or any neighbour over pensionable age.

The countdown to the next full moon was painfully slow at first but then time appeared to accelerate. The DNA testing was less than half complete so the police, backed up by an absurd bylaw, actually placed the town on an official 'limitation of movement' which they were too cautious to call a curfew. Pubs and shops were closed by nine. People were advised to stay at home and not venture out in their cars. Compliance was close on one hundred percent. It was effectively a lockdown, where the virus was murder.

The moon, maybe making a solemn point, rose provocatively early that evening. Its stolen light furnished the sea with a silver pathway from horizon to shore, but few were around to see it. The air became taught and hard as the temperature sank. Frank diligently went around the house, checking every entrance was securely bolted.

He was disturbed to find that the lock on the side door was slipping and would present no problem for a motivated intruder. Frank unscrewed the lock and took it to his shed for closer inspection. Maisie, his oldest daughter, already bored of the restrictions, soon joined him. She couldn't understand why her father was fussing so about the locks when all the murders to date had been committed in the open: this murderer was not a house caller. Frank said that he wasn't taking any risks. On that, he asked her to pass him the box of screws.

As she lifted it a locket fell to the ground. She quickly picked it up, teasing him about who it was intended for. Frank was as surprised as she was. She opened the locket and there was a tiny picture of a young couple.

"Wait a minute," she said, moving it into the moonlight which was beaming through the shed window. "This is the couple, the ones who were killed last October. What's it doing in our shed? How did it get here?"

As her father grabbed it to take a look, he let out a gasp, as he too recognised the couple. A shadow passed over his face as he held the locket tight and, with it, a million images shot into his mind, gruesome images of blood and teeth, of torn flesh and severed limbs.

In the split second after his daughter said they must phone the police, Frank bit into her throat, her startled face showed that she could make no sense of what was happening. Her last picture of the world was of her father visibly changing in front of her, the sudden growth of hair, the elongated teeth now dripping with her blood, the piercing blackness of his eyes. Throwing her dying body to one side, he was seized with a hunger so deep it was painful. He

95

wanted more and, taking the short path back to the house, silently slid in through the unsecured side door.

The howling the neighbours reported the following day was put down to kids messing about, until, that is, their neighbour knocked on Frank's door.

WANC
Diane Narraway

"It had been several years since the first werebeast came forward seeking help. Of course, there was no real help available: medical, holistic, psychiatric or otherwise. That didn't stop the reputable trying to find a cure, nor did it stop the less scrupulous from taking money from those desperately wanting to be cured. In the end, the only sensible conclusion was that more research was necessary, therefore a new, very high-tech research centre was built. This was, for all intents and purposes, a very luxurious and extremely expensive prison. A way of containing those more dangerous werebeasts while the scientists and doctors worked on a cure—or more accurately cures. It was very quickly deemed unlikely that one cure would work for every species.

As is often the way, people are curious, and their curiosity is cruel. Over time, viewing panes were installed and these luxurious prisons became little more than ultra-expensive zoos. Prisons or zoos, it didn't much matter what you called them, if you were deemed a dangerous werebeast they were a non-negotiable, Life Until Cured sentence. For those caught harbouring a werebeast, the sentence could be just as long. The following story is an account of the events following the disappearance of prima ballerina, Sylva Starling ..."

"My story, I'm Reuben by the way, is really about a friend of mine—a rather annoying man of average height, slightly overweight, and somewhat self-important. But then, he is single, so perhaps that's why—if he had someone else to care about he might be different.

I met him—John, that's his name, even his name is dull—at work. I run a dance studio, Reubenz. I mostly teach classical ballet and John had a bit of a 'fan-scination' with a very famous principal ballerina, Sylva Starling—he was a proper 'fan girl'. He came to my studio wanting to learn all her dance moves and offering to generously compensate me. So, I went home and studied hours of Sylva Starling footage. Lord knows how many ballets that woman has been in or how many hours of it I watched.

To be honest, he'd probably watched more hours than I had, I reckon he probably knew her moves better too, but not the technique. That's where I came in. And that's where our friendship began.

Sylva Starling was pretty reclusive. I mean, she never appeared in the papers, she was never the subject of gossip, yet everyone, dancer or otherwise, knew her name. Perhaps she was more famous for what wasn't known about her rather than her actual talent, which was indeed undeniable. Don't get me wrong, I was a fan too, I just wasn't quite as obsessed as John.

He came every other day and trained hard, and for the first few weeks our sole topic of conversation was Sylva. Of course, I thought this was odd, well, probably quirky, like I said, he was like a starstruck teenage girl. If I hadn't been gay myself I might've thought he was—I am, and he definitely wasn't.

Over time, I discovered he worked as an accountant, with a fair number of famous clients on his books. He also had an ex, a woman named Annie, and they had a daughter, unsurprisingly named Sylvia. I assumed that was as close as his ex would let him get to Sylva. I can't imagine I would want a child named after someone my partner was infatuated with.

I met her once, his daughter. She was 14 years old and a slight little thing, coquettish and very spoilt.

He told her he'd bought her a gift. It was a pastel faux flower arrangement in a ceramic foot. It sounds grim but it was actually quite a pretty ornament. She just said 'Thanks Daddy, but I'm not sure I can carry it upstairs'. Is she for real? It weighed a pound at most, and yes, Daddy carried it upstairs for her. Like I said, spoilt!

Anyway, I guess my story really starts the night Sylva Starling vanished, which normally would be much harder to determine. However, on this occasion she had been out with friends, and had been photographed by the pap. By the time this happened, we—John and myself—had become good friends, so perhaps I shouldn't have said all that about him to start with, but he was damn annoying at times. And I feel I need to get that across.

I phoned John as soon as I saw the morning news, but he was already in bits. I told him they said she left with a man, but he said he doubted it, and that she often walked home on her own. Apparently it helped her keep fit and gave her thinking time.

I asked him how he even knew all that, perhaps somewhat unnecessarily. After all, John wasn't actually saying anything that wasn't already known about her. I mean, there was some info about her on social media, it just wasn't as much as other celebs, nor was it as easy to find. Social media is always the last playground of anybody who's nobody.

Anyway, he said 'I just do', then the phone clicked, and he was gone. I knew he had his daughter some weekends, so I left him to it, just in case. He didn't sound good though. Don't get me wrong, she would leave a gaping hole in my life, but then John is different, especially where Sylva Starling is concerned.

He called in the next day to apologise for putting the phone down on me, but I assured him no apology was necessary. It appeared she had left with a man and that she had actually been missing for several days. I had no idea how he knew this stuff, I presumed he was president of the Sylva Starling Fanclub so had inside intel. Truth is I didn't care, I was lapping it up. Let's face it, goss is goss. Right? He always had a little bit more info here and there to drip feed me with, and like I said, all goss is good. I'm gay; we practically invented gossip. Well, us and women. Eventually, probably longer than it should've taken, I reported him.

He was my friend, but the info he had was becoming a little unsettling, and he had his daughter there. In truth, I felt he may be on the verge of a breakdown. He kept rambling about werebeasts. I have plenty of clients who chat about were stuff all the time, but John wasn't one of them. He had gone, almost overnight, from being Sylva Starling's number one 'fan girl' to a werebeast rights activist. They couldn't be more different. So, like I said, I reported him to the authorities.

If I'd known, would I have done it differently? Definitely not, I mean some of these creatures really are lethal. I wouldn't want to be ripped to shreds by a werelion or werebear, and John wouldn't have wanted that either, especially not for his little Sylvia. I may have thought her spoilt but he clearly adored her.

Still, one man's brat is another man's angel, and who am I to judge? I think I would have tried to help him a different way, a better way, but I didn't know that option existed then.

When I phoned the authorities, my intention was getting my friend the help he needed to recover the plot he had so obviously lost. Which authorities? The medical ones of course. I wanted him helped not arrested.

And yes, I know he was arrested, and no, I haven't visited him. I'm too ashamed, and a bit angry with him. If he'd trusted me enough to tell me the truth then maybe it needn't have come to this.

What did happen? I called the medical authorities two weeks after her reported disappearance, and just so it's clear, I contacted the local shrink. I explained the situation as best I could. My unprofessional diagnosis, such as it was, was that a Sylva Starling 'totally loco fangirl' had been tipped over the edge by her disappearance a few weeks back. Since then, said 'totally loco fangirl' had become a fully-fledged, fully paid-up werebeast rights activist. No, not just a supporter, that I might've got, but an active member of WRA, pronounced rah, like a growl. Good acronym, but lousy intentions.

Having made the call, I envisioned them paying him a visit, contacting Sylvia's mother, Annie, assuming Annie was there, and then assessing him before arranging a treatment plan. After all, they aren't monsters.

Had I ever been to John's house? Yes, when I met his daughter. It was just how I imagined, reeking of Sylva Starling. Like I said, he was infatuated with her. I guess looking back, considering what he must have earned, it wasn't over showy; more tasteful and delicate, a bit like his daughter, Sylvia, I guess.

Do I know what actually happened? Yes, but I wish I didn't. I suppose more accurately, I know what I was told happened.

The local shrink arrived and was refused entry, which left them no choice but to phone the police. The police arrived, at which point he answered the door in tears, with his hands out ready for cuffing. They took Sylvia into care, although I'm not sure why, but I presume they contacted her mother to get her later, and of course, they took Sylva Starling. I knew he was unhinged but holding Sylva captive with a live werebeast in the house, well, that's next level unhinged. Info like that is a game changer where friendships are concerned. Still in an ironic way, he'll get the help he needs, just in a different setting.

Do I want to see what really happened? I thought I did know. There's a film? Why didn't anyone show me this before?"

The film began with the arrival of the local psychiatrist. They did knock and there was no answer, so they contacted the local authorities. And, as was stated, the police did knock, a couple of times but on no occasion was there an answer.

After 3 attempts armed police forced their way into the house, with a shoot first, ask later policy. On the other side of the door was Sylvia with Daddy beside her holding her hand. Both father and daughter were standing in front of Sylva Starling, who was being held in a cage behind them. Both reached for the sky as soon as the door burst open. The police cuffed both— at this point they didn't ask questions, they simply cuffed them and threw them into the back of the van. They remained there, with an armed guard, while the house was searched and a werebeast handling unit removed Sylva Starling.

Now, do you see? Sylva had been caged in John's house. Although it was a reinforced cage with armoured steel plates, which protected her on the full moon, she was what is referred to as 'unchained'. There were two large room-sized cages, which were halved on full moon nights, to prevent damage to either her or her belongings. Most of the month Sylva was free to roam the house and her ballet commitments were upheld, just strategically booked. Sylva wasn't missing as such, she was at home."

"At home?" Reuben quizzed.

"You really don't know anything do you? Still, you were right about one thing, you should be ashamed.

John wasn't a ... what was it you called him? A 'totally loco fangirl'. He was her husband, you damned fool. That's how he knew so much about her, and of course Sylvia was named after her mum. That's why they took her into care, and by care, read 'Werebeast Analysis Neoresearch Centre', or WANC for short.

They took Sylva there too, and she wasn't being kept in the house with a werebeast, she was the damned werebeast. John was the man she was seen with the night of her disappearance. He came to get her after she had rung him. She had gone to the toilet and there was a recently transformed wereleopard in there. As is so often the case with these tragic creatures, they hate themselves, if not instantly, certainly after a short time. The thing is, most of the time these people are human, like me and you, many successful. They aren't murderers, but during the full moon it changes. This leopard had gone there with the sole intention of leaping out of the window to her death."

"But why?" Reuben shook his head partially with disgust, but mostly with confusion.

"A farewell dinner with her husband and children. Something Sylva and her family will never be able to do. The wereleopard executed her plan as intended but had sadly caught Sylva with her claw in the process. We know this because we found the wereleopard the next day. This was followed by John contacting us. We helped his family build a sensible, not ideal, but better than WANC, enclosure, so they could remain a family a bit longer.

Obviously watching, or even hearing your loved one struggling to transform is heartbreaking, and John tried to confide in you, but you just enjoyed the 'goss'. No, not all gossip is good. So, as a result of your actions, Reuben, John will live out his days alone in prison with murderers, rapists and other undesirables. Can you see a man who took ballet lessons to help his wife train, as a man equipped to deal with Cat A prisoners? Cos I damned sure can't. As for his family, the one he doted over, well, Sylvia and her mother will be WANC lab rats, in the search for a cure they don't really want."

"Why don't they want it?" Reuben asked.

"Dollar, my boy, dollar! WANC earn far too much money from their freakshow zoo. There is talk of them even introducing a petting zoo. Makes my skin crawl just thinking about it. And no, I'm not a werebeast, but my son is, and I am a founder member of Werebeasts are People, W.A.P!

We aren't campaigning for werebeasts to be released into the wild, you damned idiot. We campaign for the right for them to live in safe enclosures, like Sylva Starling. Now, I'd like you to meet my son. And don't look so worried, after all, we're not monsters."

ALPHA'S DAUGHTER
Kate Knight

There was nothing better, more exhilarating and wholesome than the feeling of the cold wind dancing through your winter coat, while running along with the pack. The soft, powdery snow crunched under our paws and the rich smell of the fresh pine tingled our senses. I loved being in my pack, they were loyal and fair and I, being the Alpha's daughter, had privileges that allowed me to run by my father's side while hunting.

We had been aware of a gathering of boar in the area; the smell of their droppings was enough to make our eyes water. We could also smell the pungency of a heavily pregnant sow or two among them, which was ready to expel a plentiful litter. Nothing was more juicy and tender than a week old boarlet, their bones were still soft to chew and biting down through their flesh required next to no effort. Of course, we had to contend with the angry mother, but our pack was strong and our techniques had been passed down through generations and never failed us. Boars were fast, but they were fat and clumsy and cared more for filling their own stomachs than watching out for the likes of us.

My father had caught hold of their scent a few weeks ago, but was eager not to hunt them too soon. We were still devouring the elk that we brought down a few days previously; the snow kept the meat fresh for longer than usual. It was when the sun warmed the land enough to thaw the snow, that my father sniffed the air outside of our den. The smell of fresh boarlets and their fragrant afterbirth carried on the breeze, teasing our taste buds for far too long. At last our alpha gave us the signal that it was time to gather for the hunt. This land is where I grew up, where my mother taught me how to hunt efficiently, but my father taught me how to hunt the way our ancestors did for generations. The pack was carefully positioned with the strongest females, including myself, at the front, leading the way along with our alpha. The other males gathered either side of the older and younger pack members to protect them from predators. It was the best way to traverse this terrain as you could never tell what lay beneath the snow, or indeed, what sharp-toothed enemy hid within the undergrowth.

As we drew closer, the smell became stronger. My father stopped dead in his tracks.

"What is it, what's wrong?" I enquired.

"Can you not smell it? Something is different."

My father pointed his snout into the air and took a good sniff. I followed suit, hoping that I could impress him with my heightened sense of smell. I took a few deep breaths and closed my eyes, while I tried to distinguish what the strange odour was. I could smell the boar, the pungent smell of the dung and something very different. A smell that I didn't recognise. It was like a floral smell but with a hint of old hide, something metallic yet with a splash of strong mint and onion; a strange richness that I was wholly unfamiliar with.

"What is that father?" I asked, disappointed at myself for not being able to put a name to the strange odour.

"It is man, daughter. Man has come to our land and has taken some of the young boar and chased off the rest. I'm afraid we must turn back."

Our alpha looped back in the direction we came and retraced his steps to the den.

Later that evening I found my father outside alone, gazing at the mountains in deep thought. I walked beside him, sat down on the chilled ground and rubbed my ear on his shoulder. I had a question on the tip of my tongue, that I had been holding onto all day. A question that I had a feeling that my father was waiting anxiously for.

"What is Man?"

Father sighed. "Man is a creature, unlike any other. They are not fast or clever, but they hunt with something that we cannot outrun. It's a long weapon that sits against their

112

shoulder. They aim it at us and out from the end comes a loud bang instantly followed by a pulse of fire that pierces holes through our flesh from a great distance. Almost every time, that weapon takes a life from the pack. The last time we came across man, our alpha was taken from us. He was brave and led our pack well and kept us healthy. We were out hunting a group of deer when a man came from nowhere and released his fire. The alpha didn't stand a chance. His body hit the floor dead within moments of the bang, blood oozing from his head. We tried to attack the man, but he took down three more of our strongest and threw fire in the faces of the rest of us. Four were lost that night, three more a few days later from their injuries. We stay away from man. Do you understand me, daughter? We stay away."

I must admit that the thought of ever coming close to man terrified me more than anything. A weapon that killed from a great distance was inconceivable, how could we ever win against that?

Later that night we were all back in the den, curled up together to preserve our heat from the bitter cold. I dreamt of man; I dreamt that he came to our den and threw his fire inside while we slept. It caught hold of the bedding and the flames ignited the fur of some of our pack. I could hear them screaming as they tried to extinguish their coats, the smell of burning flesh was everywhere. In a panic they all ran through the flames and into the night, leaving me alone cowering in the far corner, unable to escape.

I woke up with a start and looked around me. All seemed well and my pack was still sleeping. The very first rays of the sun were creeping through the entrance of our cave, as the dawn made itself known. I waited until my heart had slowed from the dream and uncurled myself from my mother's warmth. With one leap I stealthily freed myself from the pack and went out to watch the sun illuminate the mountains. It was a chance to take in the very first scents of the day in the morning breeze. Maybe something new would float by and I could report my findings to the alpha. It was a chance to prove that I had a talent for sniffing out prey. I sat my rear on the grassy earth and pushed my snout into the cool air. I could smell such fragrant delights; the smell of freshly laid eggs from the big nest in the tall fir tree, the musk of a deer, the earthy scent of a bear that was too far away to be any kind of threat and the aroma of rabbits emerging from their burrows. I could smell the freshness of the snow as it thawed under the warm sun. Another scent of something different and unusual hit my snout. It smelt like a mixture of damp earth and smoke.

I heard a click from behind me. I turned in an instant, but as I did so, I heard a loud noise and my world blurred and plunged into darkness. The last sight that I saw was a silver-coloured tube with smoke wafting from the end.

I awoke in a place that was completely unfamiliar. I was afraid and weak and found it hard to lift my head. The small space was built from wood and I was trapped within, barely able to turn around on the straw strewn floor. I heard strange noises from outside, so began to howl and snarl for them to release me. I tried to call for the rest of my pack but as I did, my enclosure lifted into the air and slid across a smooth platform.

Another loud bang made me cower in fear. I peered through a small hole in the wall and to my horror, there was a man. He was talking in his own language to another man, who had something in his mouth that glowed hot with embers. He sucked the smoke into his chest before releasing it into the air. I could smell its strong odour and felt it burning my nasal passages. It made me sneeze twice. I knew that man was dangerous and alerting my pack would only bring death. I daren't do that, as living with them being harmed on my conscience would be fatal in itself. I had to escape from this place and there was no one coming to help me.

I cowered into the far corner and tucked myself into a ball. They had to open my

115

enclosure eventually, and when they did so, I'd be ready for them. I was my father's daughter; strong and brave. I just had to trust my instincts and my sense of smell.

My prison began to move over the rocky terrain in an unusual bouncing motion that made me feel quite sick. Back and forth I swayed, I tried to stand on my feet to steady myself but was quickly knocked back down. Eventually the ground became smoother. I sat upright and peeked through the small hole again. I could see the trees zoom past in a blur, much faster than I could ever run. I thought that if I was able to escape this place, that the fall to the ground alone would most likely kill me. Staying quiet and curled up in my ball was the best option for now. My scent would lead me home when my opportunity to escape arrived. I could hear the continuous droning of whatever my enclosure was travelling in and the dull chatting from my captors. Tiredness crept upon me, and still feeling the effects of whatever they gave me, I fell asleep.

I awoke to the sound of more man speaking. I could see many of them surrounding me. The smell of their glands and their uncleanliness carried for miles, leaving a trail that must have mixed with my own. One of them looked at me and began making strange noises to get my attention. I bared my teeth at him in the hope that he would go away but as I did, I heard a strange noise from behind me and felt a sharp pain in my rump. Again my eyes were forced into the darkness of sleep. For a moment, a thought struck me that this may have been my death and finally my ordeal was over. I dreamt of my pack and being snuggled up next to my mother, smelling her sweet fragrance, comforting me once again.

My eyes opened expecting to be back home, but my gaze was greeted with a glaring, white light that burned my eyes. I was in a new enclosure, a cage with silver bars that criss-crossed all around me, under my feet was fresh straw. Looking in on me was a strange female man in a white coat. She was looking at me with her teeth bared, clicking on my enclosure with her small transparent stick. My head was still spinning, but I used what strength remained in me to lunge at her. My cage fell to the ground and the female man screamed and left through a gap in the wall. My paw was trapped between the floor and my enclosure. I tried to pull it free but every time I moved the pain grew, causing me to scream. Eventually the female man came back with another man and they moved my enclosure back to where it was and freed my paw. I was relieved but still terrified. Why wouldn't they just kill me? Why were they torturing me like this? What had I done?

I was in the middle of an open space with smooth powder-blue walls in a tiny enclosure. I had no shelter, nowhere to hide, no food or water. The space was filled with strange boxes

117

that flashed with lights and made unfamiliar noises. Man surrounded my cage and they spoke to each other in a calm manner, like I wasn't even there.

As I gazed around, a man came up behind me and stabbed something sharp into my rump. I expected to fall back to sleep like the last few times, but this time was different. Slowly my rump began to tingle, the tingling travelled down my hind legs and reached my back paws. After a while I lost all control of my back end; it had become completely numb, like it no longer belonged to me. The tingling kept travelling up my spine, taking with it all function. My body was becoming limp and there was nothing I could do. My bowels let loose filling the air with the smell of my own excrement, my bladder spilled onto the ground. I had lost all control of everything. All that was any use to me was my senses. I could see everything around me, could hear them speaking and still smell the dangers that were surrounding my enclosure.

The female man poked my shoulder through the bars with her transparent stick, but I could not feel anything. She showed her teeth again and opened the door. Her hand cautiously came towards me. I went to bite her flesh, but my body wouldn't respond. My eyes widened with terror and I could feel my chest pounding as the female man and her companion pulled me from my enclosure. They lifted me through the air and laid me gently onto a flat, cold slab. All the time, the two were speaking in their language while they shone lights into my eyes and rammed strange things down my throat. My lungs inflated and deflated by themselves as strange boxes around me made whirring and beeping sounds. I could smell odours that were unfamiliar, not like any animal or anything natural. They pierced my skin with tiny metal tubes and drew out blood from my body. The man did something unexpected, he began caressing my ear, as though he was trying to bring me comfort. The terror I felt was indescribable, it would take more than an ear rub from him to settle my nerves. I was being killed slowly by these barbaric man creatures. All that I could do was hope that the end would come swiftly.

Another man arrived by my side. This one carried a black leather box with a handle. He laid it by my head and opened it up. Inside was a strange, blue thing with a silver tube attached to one side. The female man used a shiny item with buzzing teeth on my leg, removing a patch of hair with ease. The other man fumbled my skin then pierced a vein, pumping the blue liquid into my leg. After, he covered my wound with some brightly-coloured skin, pulled the long item from my throat and the three of them lifted my limp body back into the cage and secured it tightly. They walked out of the space and the lights went out instantly.

I lay in the dark, on the cold straw. My whole body tingled, but I felt no pain. I was panting wildly, I was thirsty. So, so thirsty. I knew that if I didn't drink soon then I would be in trouble. As time went on, my body started to feel like my own again, all apart from the strange burning sensation, where the blue liquid was pushed into me. All around me lights flickered and strange eyes looked into my cage. I was exhausted and felt that it was finally safe to close my eyes. Hopefully I would be given water when the man came back.

I was awoken with a pain that shot through my body. Something was wrong. Everything throbbed and I could do nothing but scream. I felt my bones shattering and re-forming, my muscles tearing and twisting. My head felt like it was crushing inwards, then expanding at the same time. My eyes bulged then sunk back into the sockets. One by one I could feel and hear my ribs snapping as my chest expanded. I expected that my body was about to explode and I braced myself for the end, but the end of my life never came. Eventually the pain began to subside and I was able to relax a little. What was that blue liquid that they pushed into my leg? I closed my eyes and listened to the thumping in my chest, as it gradually slowed down to a more comfortable pace and my insides settled into a more natural position. It felt cramped in my enclosure, like somehow the walls had grown smaller. I tried to stretch out but I was restrained.

I looked around the space that I was in. The lights still blinked and the strange eyes still watched over me. Something inside clicked, an anger that I had never felt before; and a fire that raged in me. I wanted the man dead for taking me away from my pack, I wanted to tear out their throats and eat their insides. My sense of smell seemed more intense, their sweat from the other room filled my snout. I could smell the freshness of the air far above me, I could smell the rain falling on the roof and hear the sound of the water seeping through the earth deep beneath my feet. I needed to get out of that place before they did anything else to me.

I pushed on the entrance of my enclosure, which gave way with ease. Freedom was in my sights. As I stretched my limbs, I felt incredible. I felt stronger, my eyesight was clearer than it had ever been, but I was thirsty, so bloody thirsty. I threw my snout in the air and let out a deep, rumbling howl that rattled through the thick walls and travelled far into the distance. A yellow flashing light came on that almost blinded me and every way out of that place was blocked up with thick metal slabs that slammed to the ground. A loud shrieking hit my ears from a black box on the wall but I instinctively leapt up and tore it down. I could hear mans panicked voices and the sweet smell of fear. They knew that I had my senses homed in on them. They would pay for what they had done to me, they would pay with their lives.

With a single swipe, the wall crumbled at my feet, every boundary made to keep me prisoner was no match for my strength. Man hid from me, pointing their weapons but they were not powerful enough to take me down, their death bounced off my skin without even breaking my hair. Man could run, but they were not fast and certainly not clever. One man stood before me with a big weapon and a face of false bravery. I scooped him up in my paw and bit off his head. The bones were soft and the flesh tasted like the wild boar. It was juicy and sweet, so I devoured the rest of the carcass. One by one I quenched my insatiable thirst on these dumb creatures with their measly weapons.

I followed my nose towards the freshness of the air, crumbling walls, leaving rubble and fire in my wake. Finally I was free, my snout hit freedom and the coolness of the rain drenching my coat felt amazing. My belly was full and my thirst satisfied. My rage dulled and I began to feel more like me again. Straight away, I caught hold of my own scent and followed it back to my pack. I ran faster than I had ever run before, transforming my surroundings to a blur. My scent had left a trail that did not falter in the rain.

Sooner than I expected I was back in familiar surroundings, with the same scents

122

that I was raised with. I felt elated with excitement to see my pack again and rushed back to the den. As I approached, another smell hit my snout, a smell that only indicated death. The smell of fire and burning flesh had taken over the sweet smell of my family. I peered into the darkness to be faced with the charred remains of my entire pack. I sat my rump on the ground and howled with the pain in my heart and hoped that any survivors might reply. Not a sound was heard.

I howled a second time, this time louder and deeper, my echoes travelled further, tearing through the mountains and forests. I had almost given up hope when I heard a rustling from behind me and a feeble whimper. It was my mother's sister. She had been injured badly by the weapons of man.

"What happened here?" I asked. "What happened to the pack?"

She looked up at me with fear. She sniffed the air to find my scent.

"Are you the alpha's daughter?"

"I am."

"I'm so glad you are alive. It was man, they came and set fire to the den when we were sleeping. I managed to escape but they caught me, and left me for dead. Please. I'm in so much pain. Please end my life so I can be with my family."

I could see the pain that she felt, it was like I could see through her body, her wounds glowed bright red. I took her throat in my jaw but as my teeth pierced her skin, I just couldn't do it. She was all I had left. It was selfish, but there is no greater fear for a wolf than the thought of being alone. We are pack animals and cannot survive for long on our own. If she was to live just one more day then I was going to take it. I used my renewed strength and dagger-like claws to dig out a new den close by, I lined it with soft bedding and took my aunt in my jaws and laid her down. I curled my body around her for warmth and fell asleep.

"Alpha. Wake up. I smell man."

I opened my eyes to the face of my aunt staring down at me. She was healthy and strong, as strong as I was. Her size had doubled and every wound on her body had healed. I was so happy to have her with me. She explained that when my jaw pierced her throat, she felt my power seep into her body. From that instant she could feel herself changing. She healed in no time and felt more powerful than ever before.

That day we hunted for our favoured prey to quench our thirst. It was not wild boar or elk that we desired but something sweeter, a treat that was in abundance. Their bones were easy to digest and their flesh tasted like wild boar, but a little different. They are in abundance in these lands, usually gathered in packs of their own, living in strange stone boxes, covering themselves in the pelts of animals as they are bald and susceptible to cold.

We soon tracked down another wolf pack, relatives of our own. We gifted them all with a small nip on the rump that healed in a few short hours, giving them immense strength, stamina and immortality. The old grew young and the young grew wilder. We are now a strong pack of over one hundred, raising our young in a place where man once flourished. Food is in abundance and our space is plentiful. We no longer fear predators, sickness or even death, as we are yet to see death come for any of us, despite the growing power of man's weapons. Every morning I sit on the top of the mountain and let out a call for the memory of my family and look down upon the new family I have created.

We are the Gods of this land and I am their alpha.

THE TROPHY
Ron Miller

I only wish that all the jokes you've heard about traveling salesmen were true. It's crossed my mind more than once, I can tell you, that I've never gotten my share of farmers' daughters. In fact, I've never even met a farmer's daughter. I'm not even sure I'd know what to do if I did. Probably try to sell her the latest, 1947 line of Lustron porcelain-clad steel siding, I suppose.

I do know that porcelain-clad steel siding wasn't the first thing on my mind when the black-haired girl opened the door in answer to my knock. But then, she was no farmer's daughter, either. Tall, slender as one of those Vogue models but a lot healthier-looking, with startlingly wide-set green eyes in a face as white as a #2 Vanilla Creme Premium panel. It seemed to take her a second to focus on me, as though it were an effort to swing those wide-set glims onto something standing as close to her as I was, like a Navy rangefinder taking aim at an enemy cruiser.

"Yes?" she asked, pleasantly enough, though there was something about her voice that sent a shiver down my back. But a good shiver, if you get what I mean.

"Good morning," I said. "My name is Barrow, Creighton Barrow. I represent the

Lustron company, manufacturers of the finest porcelain-clad steel home siding on the market today. I have an appointment with a Mr. Helsinki—"

"Isn't that nice," she interrupted with what seemed to be genuine enthusiasm.

"I'm Gayl. That's with a Y but no E. It's Armenian. Please come in. I'm sure my—husband—will be delighted to hear what you have to say about your splendid product."

She stood aside to let me in, but I passed close enough to smell her. She wore a strange perfume; musky and earthy. She smelled a little like a pet shop but I liked it. I thought about saying something, but figured I'd better concentrate on my job. If she wasn't the one who paid the bills around there, flattering her wasn't going to get me anywhere.

She closed the door behind me and, with a gesture, indicated that I should follow her, which I did and was glad of it. Her swaying hips reminded me of the slow, sinuous undulations of a cobra.

She led me to pair of sliding doors. She opened the doors just wide enough to allow her to lean into the room beyond and say, "Arno, there's a man here to see you."

She must have gotten a positive answer because she stepped aside, opened the doors all the way and, with a smile, gestured for me to go on in. I hefted my sample case—porcelain-clad steel is no featherweight, you understand—and did.

What a room! I'd never seen anything like it, at least not since my last visit to the Natural History Museum, and that had been when I was a kid. There must have been five hundred stuffed animals in the place if there was one, and there was. Every level surface had some sort of furry, scaly or feathered creature sitting on it, while the walls were covered from floor to ceiling with heads mounted on big wooden plaques. Dozens and dozens of glassy-eyed faces were staring down at me from every direction, making me feel uncomfortably like a participant in some strange spectator sport, or maybe the victim in a car accident as a crowd of rubber-neckers gathered around to gawk at the mess.

What I had taken at first to be a stuffed grizzly bear, whimsically decked out in a red velvet smoking jacket and cravat, startled me by removing a cigar from its mouth, grinning like a demon and extending a hairy paw toward me.

"Good evening, Mr. Barrow!" it said in a very good imitation of Wallace Beery. "I very much appreciate your coming at such a late hour."

There's hardly any need for me to describe Helsinki any further, other than to say he looked as though someone had told Max Baer he ought to audition for the part of

Mephistopheles in a revival of Faust, if Faust is the play I'm thinking of. His big hairy hand engulfed mine like a badger sucking down a mouse as an after-dinner mint.

He was one of those big, hearty manly men who are so aggressively masculine you wonder what they keep in their underwear drawers to dance around in when the doors are locked and the shades drawn. But to keep this short, if you think of the gypsy in Walt Disney's Pinocchio, you'll pretty much have the right impression.

"Glad you could come! Glad you could come!" he roared, drawing me across the room like a little red wagon. "I was afraid, when I called your office, they wouldn't have anyone to send out on such short notice."

"I always check in before calling it a day," I said. "It's often paid off for me."

"Well, I'll be betting you'll be thinking you hit the jackpot today, my friend. Did you take a look at my house as you came up?"

Of course I had. The place was as big as the main top at Barnum & Bailey and just about as tasteful. But I said, "Sure did, Mr. Helsinki. Beautiful layout you got here, mighty fine!"

"You bet your sweet life it's fine. Biggest damn house in the tri-county area. Can I get you a drink? You look like a scotch-and-soda man to me."

Any sort of alcoholic beverage makes me break out, but I said, "Sure thing, Mr. Helsinki. It's after six so I guess I can sort of consider myself kind of off duty. But just a small one, please, with lots of ice. I got to keep my wits about me if I'm going to be doing business."

"Smart fella," he said, ho-ho-hoing like a department store Santa Claus. "Plenty smart. But a quick jolt never hurt a real man. Here you go." he bellowed, shoving a tumbler full of amber liquid into my hand. "Here's to good hunting."

"Um, yes, to good hunting," I replied, making the most enthusiastic salute I could with my glass. If I drink this thing, I thought, I'll wake up in the morning with blisters all over my face the size of biscuits. I took a sip and carefully set the tumbler onto the glass-topped bar.

"Now, Mr. Helsinki—" I began, hoping I could distract him from the subject of alcohol.

"Arno!" he boomed. "Arno! We're all friends here. Just a couple of bluff, hearty fellows talking some plain, down to earth business talk."

"Uh, yes. Well, um, Arno ... my office told me that you were interested in cladding your entire, um, house in Lustron porcelain-clad steel siding."

"You got that right, my friend. You got that right. The whole shebang—top to bottom, side to side. Every damn square inch."

131

Holy smoke! I tried to keep the glitter of sheer avarice out of my eyes. The entire house. Why, the thing must have a surface area measurable in acres.

"That'd be fine, just fine," I managed to say as non-nonchalantly as I could, if nonchalant means what I think it does. "An excellent decision, Mr ... um, Arno, an excellent decision, indeed! Lustron porcelain-clad steel panelling is the best investment a man can make in his home."

"Tough stuff, ain't it?"

"Oh, yes indeed, indeed it is. Here, let me show you a few samples."

I scrambled to get my case open before he could realise that I was ignoring my drink. He wasn't ignoring his, I noticed. In fact, he was pouring himself another pint as I undid the latch and revealed the samples. I could tell that even a big brute like Helsinki was impressed, as well he should be. The gleaming squares of porcelain-clad steel looked as brilliant and clean and inviting as ice cream. I would have said jewels, except that jewels aren't normally opaque and four inches square. No, ice cream was the simile that always came to my mind, if simile is the word I want. Cool, glimmering, smooth and in all the colours ice cream comes in and more. I took one of the gleaming tiles from the case and handed it to Helsinki.

"Great heavens! It looks like marzipan but it's as heavy as armour plate."

"You bet it is, Arno. A genuine Lustron porcelain-clad steel tile is as tough as the skin of any battle cruiser. Rain, hail, B-Bs, baseballs, you name it, Lustron can take it. That finish, sir, may look as fragile as the varnish on a lady's dainty fingernail but I can tell you right now that it'll outlast the house you put it on. You'll never have to paint again—just hose 'er down every now and then and she'll be as bright and pretty as new."

"Amazing! And tell me ... this is proof against hail, baseballs—as you say—but what about animals?"

"Animals?"

"Yes, you know ... the tearing, rending tusks of the enraged wild boar, the razor-sharp talons of the blood-maddened puma, the scimitar-like claws of the berserk Kodiak ... you know, that sort of thing."

"Well, I do know that bullets will bounce off it. We tried that and you can see the amazing results in our promotional film, Lustron Beauty versus Tommy Gun Lead. It's a wonderful little movie. Shows how Dillinger would be alive today if he'd only hidden out in a Lustron-clad house."

"Excellent! This gets better every moment."

"Yes, not even one of those monsters up there," I said, gesturing grandly toward the snarling, glassy-eyed heads that loomed on the

133

walls that surrounded us, "could get through a Lustron-clad wall."

"Not even the horn of the mighty rhinoceros?"

"Be like a can opener trying to unzip an aircraft carrier."

"Not even the gleaming, ivory tusks of a charging rogue elephant?"

"He'd bounce off it like a ping pong ball."

"Well, I think you've sold me, Mr. Barrow. Indeed I think you have."

"Not that you would ever have to worry about such things, not in rural Illinois, at any rate," I said, perhaps a little too lightly, the sip of whiskey I'd had earlier obviously having gone to my head.

"Do you hunt, Mr. Barrow?"

"Pardon? Hunt? No," I said, a little puzzled by the sudden change in topic. I hoped he wasn't thinking twice about the sale and determined to get him back on track before too much momentum was lost, if momentum is the word I want. "I'm afraid I'm strictly a city boy. Never hunted for anything wilder than a parking space."

"Hmm ... I've hunted all over the world ... as you can see. There hasn't been a creature worth hunting that hasn't fallen before my eagle eye, steady nerves and lightning-like trigger finger. The mighty bear—brown, black and grizzly—the bighorn sheep, the cape buffalo, water buffalo and bison, wildebeest, zebra and elephant—African and Asian—swans, ducks, bantengs, the kangaroo, crocodile, wild pig and wild groat, the caribou, chukar, goose and grouse—both black and red—hare, elk, peccary, muskrat and moose, the pronghorn antelope, wild boar, turkey, pheasant and woodcock, deer—red, roe, fallow, sika, muntjac and Chinese water—walrus, seal, polar bear and whale. I suppose you can imagine how boring this became after a while?"

"Easily."

"It was then I discovered the existence of an entirely new world of hitherto unknown game animals. What a revelation it was. It was like discovering a parallel universe, one which exists alongside our own but entirely unknown, unperceived by everyone. Unperceived, yes, but hinted at in the old myths and legends."

I had no idea what he was talking about. I glanced at my watch and saw that it was getting to be very late. The last glow of sunset had faded and, through the east window, I could see the milky glow of the full moon about to rise. If Helsinki kept this up I wouldn't be back to my hotel before midnight. Still, it wouldn't pay to be too abrupt so I decided to humour him for a few more minutes before turning the conversation back to Lustron porcelain-clad steel siding.

"You mean like the Loch Ness monster?" I asked.

"Something like that. But better and infinitely more dangerous, more cunning, more worthy of my mighty skills as a hunter."

"Well, I can't—"

"You are familiar, of course," he said, his voice suddenly dropping to a conspiratorial whisper, "with werebeasts?"

"You mean like Lon Chaney?"

"Pfft! Lon Chaney is as a tame Pekingese compared to the mighty creatures I'm talking about. A mere lap dog. Imagine human beings with inhuman strength and speed, imagine animals with human cunning and cruelty. There you have the werebeasts."

"There's more than one kind?"

"Study the folklore of every nation and you'll find tales of were animals that will keep you awake and wide-eyed for weeks. Not only your common or garden-variety werewolf, but werebears, weresnakes, werebats, wereboars and werecats of every kind—you name it. Why, the Irish even have wereseals, of all things."

"Wereseals, eh? Well, well! Think how pretty a seal would look, surrounded by glistening white Lustron..."

"It's taken years and years but I've gotten them all. Oh, the stories I could tell you."

"And you have no idea how anxious I am to hear them, but..." I gave a subtle glance toward my watch, but Helsinki was not a man susceptible to subtleties.

"They were terrifying at first, even to me, if you can believe that. But I soon learned that I could beat them, beat them all. Soon enough, they held no further terrors for me. If anyone had any reason to be afraid, it was them, the werebeasts. But ..." He refilled his tumbler. I had lost count of how many times he had done this, but I did notice that the bottle was now empty. Helsinki looked at it rather forlornly, as though it were a brilliant child who had just brought home an F on its report card. "But," he continued, "times have changed since the middle ages. This is an age of communication and organisation. I discovered that it was no longer me against individual prey, but a prey that had unionised. I might shoot a werewolf one night, but the next day his kith and kin were telephoning and telegraphing one another—and not only their fellow werewolves, but werebeasts of any kind, all of whom had to become human some time during the day, all who were anywhere near a telephone or telegraph office. And in this day and age who is not? I would find myself on another hunt a week later surrounded by were creatures of every type, animals who would never be caught dead together in the wild were now organised against their common enemy: me. Now I think you understand my interest in your fine product, Mr. Barrow."

"The Lustron porcelain-clad..."

"Yes! Yes! I want my house to be armour-plated. I want it proof against claw, talon, hoof, antler, horn, fang and tooth."

The man was obviously insane and I wondered if it were in the cards to get his name on a contract before he went completely berserk and started snapping at my ankles and cackling like a chicken. Or even worse, as I realized that in addition to the macabre collection of stuffed heads the room was a veritable arsenal of deadly weapons. Guns of every vintage and variety, knives, swords, axes—God knew what all—filled cabinets and littered the floor. I then noticed, to my horror, that a huge pistol lay within inches of the hairy brute's trembling fist.

"Look," I said, trying to keep my voice level, "I realise this will be a big decision for you. Let me leave some of these samples with you along with a few pieces of descriptive literature. Look it all over at your leisure. Take your time. Here's my card. Feel free to call me whenever you've decided what you need. Be delighted to send one of my men out to process the contract. Delighted. Absolutely delighted."

The room had been growing dark as Helsinki had been talking, but suddenly the moon rose above the trees and a silvery light flooded through the open window. Apparently Helsinki had been distracted by our conversation since this seemed to have taken him entirely by surprise. "No!" he cried, like a

138

startled bull, and rushed to the tall window. Beyond the glass I could see dozens of tiny, glittering points of light. Fireflies, I thought. How pretty. But how unusual, too, that they would all be moving about in pairs.

"Too late! Too late! Too late!" Helsinki was shouting as he blundered around the room like a madman ... which I presumed was exactly what he was. He tore the door from one of the gun cabinets with his bare hands, flinging the shattered wood and glass to the floor. "I thought I had them fooled at last. I changed my address. I bought this place under an assumed name. I grew a beard! How? How? How so soon? They must have hired detectives."

I had pretty much realized by this point that I wasn't going to make a Lustron porcelain-clad siding sale and began edging toward the door, hoping that whatever it was beyond the window that was exciting Helsinki so much would keep him distracted from me. I threw a final glance through the window and was amazed to see the fireflies still there. Strange fireflies that didn't blink and, oddest thing of all, still moved about in pairs, like luminous dancing partners. No, I take that back. The oddest thing was that they all seemed to be moving toward the house.

The moon cleared the last branches and the room was as brilliantly lit as if someone had thrown a switch. I instinctively turned away from the window, toward the walls covered with the gruesome trophies. The hairy, scaly, feathered, armoured, brutish faces glowed in the moonlight as though splashed with phosphorescent paint. Then ...

Then they began to change.

Where there had once been decapitated boars, wolves, cats and God knows what all, there were now the heads of men. Men of all ages and races, their faces filled with fury and ... and surprise. And then I realized that there were not only the heads of men but women, too, some of them heart-stoppingly beautiful, others with the faces of degenerate hags. But worst of all were the children ...

I didn't wait to see any more of that. I bolted through the door, not really bothering to see if it were open or not, and flung myself headlong down the hall toward the front door. The latter was unlocked, thank God, and my car was still where I'd left it. As I wrenched the door open and started to clamber into the front seat I heard shots from the house, then a terrible, terrible wailing. An ululation—if ululation is the word I want—that rose and rose and rose, then collapsed into a horrible gurgle.

Before I could even begin to imagine what that had been all about, I had the engine started and was half a mile away from that damned house.

I don't know how long I drove before I realized that I wasn't alone in the car. I could hear something breathing softly in the back

140

seat. I glanced into the rear view mirror but whatever it was, was hiding behind my seat.

"Wh-wh-who ...?" I managed to croak.

"Mr. Barrow?"

It wasn't a snarl or a hiss or a growl, so I was reassured. In fact, it was a very pleasant voice indeed ... which was even more reassuring.

"Who is it?" I asked, though I was pretty sure I knew the answer already. As I glanced again in the mirror I saw a pale face rise into the glass. It reminded me, for a terrifying moment, of the moon rising into the window back at the house. But instead, it was who I thought it was: the 'ward' I'd met earlier that evening. Her face looked like a hard-boiled egg nestled in black velvet. The only colour was in her vast green eyes.

"It's me, Mr. Barrow. Mr. Helsinki's ward ..."

"Yes, of course. Uh, Gayl. But what are you doing here?"

"The same thing you are, Mr. Barrow ... escaping that awful house."

"You'd better climb into the front seat with me. I have to look at you to talk and if I keep my eyes on the mirror we're going to get killed because I can tell you right now, I'm not stopping for anything!"

"I don't blame you one little bit, Mr. Barrow," she said as she clambered over the seat back. I was astonished at the grace with which she did that—and maybe a little disappointed at the lack of leg revealed in the process. She seemed to flow over the seat like warm taffy. "Where are we going?"

"Which way is Helsinki's place?"

"Back there," she said, gesturing over her shoulder.

"Then we're going this way," I replied, pointing straight ahead.

We didn't say much to one another after that, but instead drove deeper into the night. It took a couple of hours before either of us calmed down enough to trust our thoughts to words.

"I'm sorry you had to go through that, Mr. Barrow."

"Please, call me Creighton."

"Yes ... Creighton. It must have been an awful experience for you."

"You aren't just whistling Dixie, baby! What in the hell was that all about?"

"I guess it was pretty much what Arno told you—I was listening at the door, I confess. He was a monomaniac ... and a megalomaniac at the same time. A pretty bad combination, I guess."

"I guess."

"Well, anyway, I was practically a prisoner back there. He ... he'd taken me in when my parents were killed."

"I'm sorry ..."

"I'm pretty sure he was the one who killed them."

"What? Why?"

"He's ... he was a collector. I suppose I was just one more specimen for him. I guess he must have thought I was beautiful."

She was all of that, all right. For all that he was a nut of the first order, I couldn't fault Helsinki on his taste. I stole a quick glance toward the girl, just to confirm my conclusion that she was the most perfectly beautiful thing I'd ever seen. She was.

We drove along like that for a couple of hours, not saying much at all. I started to slow down and pay attention to where I was going as my nerves got back to normal. And as these things happened, I became more and more aware of the girl sitting quietly next to me. I was aware of the almost phosphorescent quality of her pale skin, which was the colour of a cup of cream with a single drop of blood stirred into it, of the way her black hair glistened in the light of passing cars and street lamps, but mostly of that sweet, musky scent she had. It was almost unpleasant but never quite crossed that line. Instead, it seemed to get into my head like one of those tunes you hear and can't shake for days.

"It must be nearly dawn," she said. They were the first words she'd spoken in hours and the sound of her voice startled me. I'd forgotten how husky and sibilant it was ... or maybe I'd never noticed before. She was right, though. Dead ahead of us the sky was growing light.

"I suppose it's about time we thought about where we're going," I said. "I haven't been paying a lot of attention. We must be in the middle of nowhere."

"It doesn't matter to me. All I care about is being as far away as I can get from ... from that cage!"

I wouldn't have thought it possible to hiss a word that had no S's in it, but she managed to do it—and the vehemence with which she spat it out startled me. Scared me a little, too. I was a little surprised, too, at her use of the word 'cage'. Helsinki had a pretty swank place, as near as I could tell, so 'cage' seemed to me a little over-dramatic.

"I guess I can't imagine what Helsinki was doing to you back there."

"No, no you can't. Nor what he has done."

"It was something to do with your parents' death," I said in a sudden flash of inspiration. "Wasn't it?"

"Yes!" This time the word had an S in it and she used it. "He wanted me, wanted me desperately. He forced me to marry him. It was easily done back in the old country. But he didn't care about me ... never loved me. I was nothing but a ... a trophy wife to him. Just another trophy."

Well, I had to admit to myself I could hardly blame the man. The girl was a looker, for sure. But that was no reason for anyone to abuse her. There's never a good excuse for abusing a woman. I'm a gentleman and I know better.

"He collected were-animals; you know that now. He was obsessed with them and, to the were-world, he became a murderer. No, worse: a serial killer. A mad criminal to be hunted down and eliminated. They were determined to stop him ... and finally did, as you saw last night."

"But what could all of that have to do with you? I know you're not a were-something-or-another. I mean, we've been driving under a full moon all night and you're still you."

"My dear new friend. If there are were-animals doesn't it make sense that there must also be were-humans?"

As she turned to look at me the first rays of the rising sun topped the horizon ahead of us and fell fully onto her face. Her pale skin seemed to become incandescent, like white-hot iron, and for a moment I imagined her face melting in the glare.

"Good grief!" I said. "I had no idea that your eyes were so big and round."

"All the better to see my handsome new friend."

"Your ears, too. I never noticed before how large they are."

"All the better to listen to the wonderful things you say to me."

"And your mouth ... Holy smoke! Your teeth!"

"Oh, Creighton, all the better to eat with."

Fortunately, there was a roadside diner just around the next bend. I wasn't terribly hungry after everything I'd been through and just picked at my food, but Gayl, she ate like a wolf.

TULIP LANE
Diane Narraway

"It could have been any street, but it wasn't, it was that street. It was on Tulip Lane, one of the safest places in New Orleans, a city known for its poverty and crime. But not there, nothing ever happened on Tulip Lane, and I should know, I lived there for the first 27 years of my life. You know what? I reckon I've told this story a thousand times, and every time it chills me to the core. To be honest I'm not sure anyone ever believes me, yet I seem to have, or rather my story has, become a bit of a tourist attraction. I mean, that's why you're here isn't it? Of course, you are.

These days I'm what they call an Octogenarian, was 80 last birthday, born in the summer of 1943—too young to remember the war, and a bit too sensible to have really embraced the 60's, but I certainly embraced some of that era.

This particular night, the one in question, I'd been out with a few friends, it was Jessie's bachelorette night. It was just the four of us; Lynette, Sara, Jessie and me. We always hung out together, thick as thieves we were, ever since we were kids. It was 1969, and Neil Armstrong had just taken his one small step, and with it came a new hope. If we weren't

148

celebrating Jessie's wedding, we would've been celebrating that. It seemed the whole of New Orleans was out that night, the clubs and bars were packed, and the party had overspilled into the street; it was like Mardi gras, without the costumes.

We too, had visited several bars that night, and danced in the street, and by the end of the evening we were pretty loaded. I mean, the 60's was our era after all, so it was drugs and booze all the way. We, like everyone else, had been drinking on Bourbon Street and smoking a bit too. As always, we'd had our fair share of male interest, but it was Jessie's night. There was one who caught my eye, and I'm pretty sure I caught his too, but like I said it was Jessie's night. Of course, you wouldn't know it these days, but I was a looker back then, we all were.

It was a good five, maybe six miles to Lake Shore, but it was a beautiful evening, so we decided to walk. Once away from the neon lights, you could see almost as clear as day, with that big old moon shining down on us. I was the last one on the route, but I never minded walking the last bit alone, it gave me time to ponder the evening. On this occasion I was pondering Jem—that was his name, the man who caught my eye. We had met in Fritzels, a new bar that had become quite a hot spot, especially tonight, and he was one of many unfamiliar faces. He had a way about him, a twinkle in his eye, and the biggest smile ever, and as I meandered slowly through the park I got to daydreaming.

Now, if what I'm about to tell you had happened in the park, well now, that might've made a lot more sense I suppose. But it didn't. No Sir. It happened on Tulip Lane. On a clear night, on a small street, in the safest part of New Orleans, that's where it happened.

I reckon I'd gone 200 yards and was literally a stone's throw from our porch, when I felt something hit me from behind. Not like a blow to the head, this was as though a giant beast had leapt at me and pinned me to the ground. My heart was thumping, I've never been more terrified, and that's when it bit me. I couldn't see anything, but I could feel it's hot breath on my neck, and the stench of rotten meat turned my stomach. I would've retched had my fear not rendered me paralysed. I was helpless, I wanted to scream, but I had no voice; it seemed fear had taken that from me too. I don't know how long I lay there, when you are that scared, seconds can seem like an eternity, and I'm sure it was only seconds before I felt its huge teeth ripping into my neck. The pain was unbearable, so much so, that I didn't notice its claws digging into my flesh, as it held me there.

Of course, I didn't die instantly, that would've been merciful, a kindness that I wasn't to be afforded. Because, believe me, I wanted to die, more than anything else, I wanted it to stop, and if that meant death, then so be it. But death didn't come. Instead I felt the blood, my blood, pumping out of my neck, some trickled down my cheek and into the corner of my mouth, it tasted vile. I had tasted my blood on a cut finger many times, but this was different it tasted rotten, in some way contaminated, unnatural, as though it wasn't mine. And perhaps it wasn't.

They say your life flashes before your eyes before you die—it doesn't. Everything just stopped, there was nothing. No bright lights, no welcoming relatives at the end of a tunnel; just darkness, all-consuming darkness. I was unable to see, hear or feel, and all I could sense was a wind whooshing past me, yet I was still, unable to move. I have never been more terrified than in those moments. Was that petrifying nothingness purgatory? Was that what it meant to be in Limbo? Or was that, as I suspect, Hell itself? Does the Devil live in that silent darkness? Perhaps he is that eerie wind whose song has no words but fills those recently passed with dread. To spend an eternity in that bleak place would indeed be a punishment, one that I would reserve for the wickedest souls. Was I that wicked?

I have no real idea how long I was dead. The doctor that resuscitated me said I was gone for 3 minutes. I can assure you it seemed much longer. I went home and tried to resume a normal life, but I'd changed. How could I not?

151

Of course, outwardly, there was no hiding my ordeal, after all my neck still bears the scars"

I pulled my collar back, just enough to reveal the ugly markings.

"My, look at your faces, you have the same expressions I've seen a thousand times. It's always the same mixture of horror and sympathy on strangers faces as they pass me by. But it wasn't just that. It was more, something deep inside me had changed. Those few moments in Hell with that eerie wind whooshing past me still haunt my dreams.

I tried counselling, of course I did. My family paid for several different counsellors and therapists. Hell, they even tried a spiritualist, but none of it helped, the dreams continued. It was as if I'd escaped the Devil's clutches and I was being constantly reminded that he would get me sooner or later. And then it happened. A year or so later another girl was brutally attacked, not in Lake Shore, but in New Orleans, and I became a hermit. I was scared to go out, scared to sleep—hell, I was just plain scared.

I knew I'd been lucky, if indeed you can call it that, the other girl didn't make it, although looking at it she may well have been the lucky one. Who can say?

It wasn't an easy decision, no Sir, but eventually, after much soul searching, I decided that having been given a second chance

152

at life I'd try and live it. I would begin by moving away somewhere quieter. And let's face it Alaska sure is quieter.

Oh, but I'm sure you are wondering what became of Jem and the girls. Quite honestly, I have no idea. Obviously Jessie got married, but my scars prevented me from being a maid of honour, and while I was invited, I wasn't asked to join the group photos. Needless to say we all grew apart, but in all honesty, when you feel the horror of death's icy touch, some things become less important.

And the beast? Oh yes the beast.

What was it? I'm sure I have no idea. I mean, for all I know it's still roaming around Lake Shore.

Was it a werewolf? Hell no. They're just made up; I think in all honesty it was probably a bear. I mean, wouldn't I be a werewolf if that was the case. That's how it works isn't it? And I definitely don't feel like a wolf.

But, I hear it is a full moon tonight, so perhaps you'd do well to stay in—just in case."

WHERE THE WILDFLOWERS GROW
Kate Knight

If you decide to go to our place, you will understand why we both loved it so much. If you walk through the southerly entrance to Nutmeg Valley, and continue straight, you will cross a cattle grid. The field beyond is home to a generous herd of Lincoln red cattle, but they are docile and mostly avoid you. Continue along the single track road until you reach the flintstone cottage with the low brick wall. In the spring, the front garden will be flush with yellow daffodils and poppies, in the summer, the roses will be blooming and the wisteria will welcome you with its lilac splendour. You need to pass the cottage to the left and continue down the yellow sand path until you see the entrance to the ancient woods. If you stick to the path, you will eventually come to a tree that appears to have the face of an old, haggard witch gazing down at you. This means that you are on the right path.

When I passed the witch tree, I only thought it polite to lift my hat and bow, as you can never quite tell these days what is rumour and what is fact. Whispers of the witch tree becoming angry and dealing out her curses have been spread around the area. The rumours have provoked all kinds of superstition. Anyway, what you do is your decision, as I know that you are sceptical of such notions.

Carry on along the path and eventually you will come across an oak tree that has been struck by lightning some time in history. It is split in two with each half charred with fire, yet its branches still stubbornly burst to life in the spring. It is at that tree that you must turn left once again, where you will find an old deer path that cuts through the tall fern. The deer have made the ground indented with their hooves and fertile due to the generous sprinkling of their droppings.

Follow this path and do not stray once. Eventually the area opens up to a clearing which looks as though it cascades in colourful wildflowers, with a small deer path snaking its way to the bottom. The trees are sparse, which allows the brightness of the midday sun to kiss the entire area with its glory, raising the most beautiful blooms from the fertile soil. In the centre is a hand-carved bench of sorts which both Celia and I constructed from a tree that had fallen in the storm of the spring three years past. It was there that we met in secret in the beginning and there where I fell on one knee and confessed my undying love for her.

If I close my eyes now, I can still smell the flowers, taste the sweetness of the summer rain and feel the warmth of the sun on my face. If I think hard enough, I can still hear my Celia humming that tune that she used to love. *I'll be with you in apple blossom time.* She would hum it only when she felt happy and content. I remember her complexion, her chocolate skin and deep brown eyes that seemed to stare into your soul. She wore her hair in a silk scarf that fell over her left shoulder. Her smile hid away the love that wooed me the first time I laid my eyes on her sweet face.

Celia was the serving girl of my sister Betty, who swiftly became her closest friend. I was the big brother who peered in on the pair through the cracks in the closet door that separated our rooms. I was the boy who climbed trees to the very top with my father's telescope, just to catch a glimpse of the girl who, to me, was the epitome of grace and beauty, as the two girls played in my sister's room. Once, I was caught looking through the crack in the door by the nanny. I was around twelve years of age. I was merely curious as to what they spoke about, secretly hoping that my name may be mentioned in a positive way. The nanny pinched her fat finger and thumb around my ear and dragged me down to the drawing room, where Mother was sewing her tapestries.

"I caught this little sir peering at his sister mam, while she was in her night dress," she exclaimed in a cruel way.

157

"Oh come now. He is just curious, that's all," Mother explained, kindly. "Fetch me the big leather bound book on the shelf, the one with the gold writing on the spine, won't you Freddy?"

The nanny stood for a few moments with her hand on her hips, as she clearly disapproved of the absence of a good hiding.

"That will be all, Agatha."

The nanny shook her head and exited the room.

The book in question was on the second shelf; I had to stand on tiptoes to reach its soft leather spine. I clasped my fingertips around the edges and gently pulled it from its resting place.

"Well done my lad, now come sit with me."

It was a rare moment that I got to spend time alone with my mother, without the disapproving looks of the servants or my father. I sat close to her right hip, my mother placed an arm around my shoulder and took the book from my grasp. She laid it down across both our laps, opened the cover and flicked past the title pages.

Her hand stopped on a page with a picture of a creature that resembled a large dog with a small child in its jaws. The moon was bright in the background and the trees cast their silhouette across the grassy terrain. My eyes widened when I noticed that one of the beast's canine teeth had punctured the chest of the lifeless child and blood oozed from the infant's dangling hand.

"What's that?" I asked, studying the grotesque creature.

"Freddy, I need to explain a few things to you. It's very important that you listen to me very carefully. The wolf in this picture is in fact your great uncle, Sebastian; he's your grandfather's uncle. The legend goes that a man named Yaroslav, a noble man from Russia, was journeying through the mountains after seeing his only son married to a princess. He was ambushed by some men seeking any treasure that he may have been hiding inside of the carriage. His men surrounded Yaroslav for his protection. Yaroslav had with him a small chest filled with Tartarian gold, but refused to part with it, even for the lives of his servants, who were all slain with spears. Yaroslav curled his body around the chest and wept.

'Leave me be, this is all I own,' he lied.

The leader approached the sobbing man and seeing that he was not armed, lay his arm across Yaroslav's back, which brought him small comfort.

'You prize that gold over the lives of the men who gave up their souls for your own. I will not kill you on this day, or take that precious cargo. The blood of your men has cursed your treasure and I no longer seek it as my own.

159

Take your gold but first I will taste your flesh,' he said.

'You will do no such ...' He did not finish his words before the man leapt forwards with lightning speed and bit into Yaroslav's cheek. The men disappeared back into the mountain, leaving Yaroslav unconscious in his carriage, still clinging to his chest, surrounded by the corpses of his protectors.

Over three days and nights, Yaroslav made his way back where he once came from. He remembered passing a village, his tired arm dragging the chest along the ground. When he arrived in the village, it was night time and the people slumbered in their beds. Yaroslav dropped his chest and took himself to the well to quench his thirst. But as he drank, the clouds were swept away by a passing breeze, revealing a bright and full moon. As the first beam touched the back of his head, Yaroslav's world fell into darkness.

In the morning, he found himself naked in a barn, covered with blood and pieces of flesh. His hair was matted and he was shivering with the cold. He found a coat hanging on a hook by the door and wrapped it around his shoulders to hide his dignity. He stumbled to the door and let in the light of day. Yaroslav could not comprehend what lay before him. The well had crumbled and fires blazed in every house. On the dirt all around him were the twisted remains of what was once the villagers.

Women, men and even the children had all been murdered, leaving no one alive. Their throats had been torn and their limbs scattered in the blood-soaked earth.

Thinking that the village must have been attacked by those who killed his men, Yaroslav dressed himself in what he could. He began his journey by foot to the next village on the back of a mule that had somehow escaped the slaughter. In what seemed like no time at all, he reached the town of Gorsk, where he was welcomed as a guest. He found his way back to his home, a few weeks thereafter.

News soon spread of the slaughter that took place in no less than three villages in the mountains of Russia. The entire incident was blamed on the Tartarians, as it was said that the first village left a clue: a bloodied chest containing Tartarian gold."

Mother looked at me, I expected she was checking that I was still paying attention.

"Freddy dear, you know that you are forbidden to play with your sister as we are afraid that she will get hurt. You are still young but incredibly strong. You see, the night that Yaroslav was bitten by that man in the mountains, he was infected by a wolf curse. Yaroslav was our ancestor, and his curse has been passed down through the generations. Not all men have the curse, but it does seem to creep up when we least expect it. The last man to have the curse was Sebastian. He thought he

161

could control it, but on this night he slaughtered an entire wedding party. They found him exactly like this, with the young child still in his jaws. They shot him and removed his head from his shoulders. He is buried in the church and surrounded with an iron cage to ensure he cannot return from the dead.

This is why we have to shut you in the old wine cellar one day of the month. We cannot risk the family. We thought that you were fortunate enough to dodge the curse like your father, but we found out that you had been touched by the curse when you were only young. Freddy, you may not remember, but you once had a twin. You were six months old when we discovered him in his crib with his throat torn. Blood was on your lips when we found you on the floor by the window."

Mother rubbed my shoulder as I tried to digest all that she was telling me. I had no clue that I had been a twin; we had few pictures back then. This made sense as to why they didn't want me near my sister. It had become normal that once a month the family would feed me well and lock me in that cellar room for the night. I had grown used to the routine and didn't think anything of it. I'd fall asleep and wake up elsewhere in the room, usually with blood under my nails and strange scratches on the walls, but I seemed to heal quicker than everyone else, so they didn't hurt at all. Never once did I think that some wolf curse had taken over me. As a matter of fact, I thought that all of the mythical creature curses were a load of nonsense. I never had a memory of those nights in the cellar, all I know is that I had to sit on the rug on the floor and close my eyes. Sometimes I couldn't sleep a wink, other times I fell asleep instantly. Whatever occurred, I always felt incredibly tired the next day.

I was born with the wolf curse, despite my family being hopeful that it had disappeared with my great uncle. My parents managed my condition the best way that they could, and despite my abnormal strength, I had a relatively normal childhood. My sister, Betty, was always with my beautiful Celia, along with an ever watchful eye from the nanny, who also happened to be Celia's mother. As I grew to be a young man, the two girls became radiant young women. My sister appeared quite mean and spoiled, despite the nanny's firmness. She wore her hair in pretty silk ribbons that matched her pretty dresses, her ringlets made her look like a China dolly. Celia on the other hand, had to wear the same plain dress that all the serving girls wore. Usually she dressed in the plain grey pinafore and matching bonnet to cover her braided hair, but by the age of 13 she had outgrown her grey garments and had begun dressing in a more mature style, which was cinched at the waist showing off her womanly figure.

One day I was in the garden digging for worms for my science lesson, when I heard a soft voice from the yew tree at the end of the garden.

"Hey Freddy, why do you look at me all the time?"

I looked to the tree to see Celia summoning me over, dressed in her nightgown and white bonnet. She was 16 at the time and I had just turned 17. I looked around to make sure we were alone and nervously made my way over to her.

"What are you doing in the garden in your night dress?" I asked the obvious yet awkward question.

"I lied to my mother. I told her I was sick. Freddy, I saw you watching me. You watch me all the time. Do I offend you?"

I don't know what came over me, maybe it was the wolf curse that gave me a mouth that spewed the truth, whether I wanted to or not.

"Because I like you, Celia. I have always liked you. I think you are the most beautiful creature on this earth." I took hold of both of her hands and smiled nervously, awaiting her reply. She appeared nervous and looked down at the ground.

"Freddy, it's not right. You don't want to like me. I'm just a servant girl. There's no place for you to be so attentive. It's just not proper. Please, you need to stop spying on me."

Celia pulled her hands away and turned to leave.

"Wait," I called. "I don't care what's proper or not. I love you Celia and I think we should be together. Please, let me hold you just once."

She turned around to face me, her nightgown was unforgiving as the sun shone behind her. I could see her body with all of its womanly curves. I rushed forward and grabbed her arm. I pulled her close to me and kissed her lips tenderly. I could feel her body relax as soon as I wrapped my arms around her. She placed her hands on my back, pulled me in closer and we embraced.

"Freddy, where are you with those bloody worms boy!"

It was my tutor calling me. I released Celia and promised her that we would meet up soon.

It was sooner than either of us realised. The waning moon was high in the sky, so my wolf curse was dormant for now. When the grandfather clock in the hallway struck midnight, I found myself outside of my room, making my way into the attic where I knew Celia was sleeping. Being a servant, she didn't have a lock on her door, which made it easy to get to her. I crept up the stairs, avoiding the creaking boards, and pushed down the handle on her door. Her candle was still lit and she was sitting upright in bed reading a book. She immediately looked up at me and smiled.

"Freddy, what on Earth are you doing here? You're going to get caught. God knows what they would do to me if they catch us," she said as she strategically pushed her bedpan under her bed with her foot.

"Don't worry, I'll be extra quiet. My parents' room is on the other side of the house and your mother has fallen asleep in her chair by the fire in the kitchen. Who will know?"

Celia thought for a moment, then pulled back her covers and invited me into her bed.

For a year I snuck up to her room and, despite a few close encounters, we were never discovered. Our romance quickly turned to complete and utter love for one another, but like all things wonderful, our affair was soon to be over. My sister was being shipped off to a boarding school for girls to learn how to be a lady. I should have enlisted into the army, but due to my condition, I was excused. I was to stay at home and watch from the top window, as my Celia was being transferred to another house. She was to become a scullery maid for one of my father's rich friends.

Life became unbearable without her. I missed her touch and the sound of her sweet voice. I felt my heart break every time I saw something that reminded me of her. After a year had passed, I managed to find an adequate dwelling of my own. It was on the condition that every month when the moon was at its fullest, I would journey back to my parents' home, so I could be locked away in their cellar while the wolf curse was upon me.

It was a small cottage on the edge of the forest that once belonged to an elderly woman, who found happiness in her garden. It was miles from anywhere and when night fell, the entire area was empty from all but wild animals. It was a perfect place to mend my broken heart in peace and quiet. During the day the area was a popular place for those who rode horses, as well as groups of ladies who would sit with a picnic and gossip about how disappointing their men are.

On this day, the weather was fine so I decided that it would be beneficial to take a walk in the woods. I tipped my hat and bowed my head to the witch tree and continued along the path towards the valley where the views were incredible. That's when I heard her, that familiar voice that I had missed so very much.

"Freddy, is that you?"

There she was, elegantly adorned in a plain yellow dress, her parasol resting on her shoulder. It was my Celia and she was alone.

I gasped. Looking around to ensure that we were away from prying eyes, I ran to her.

Celia let go of her parasol and we kissed like we had always kissed, only this time I was not prepared to let her go again.

167

Celia's new employer allowed her to have every Saturday off work. She had come to the valley armed with a book to relax in the sunshine.

"I know a place where we can both go where we can be alone. No one knows about it."

I took her hand and led her down the deer path to a beautiful spot I had found among the trees. It was a place far from any path walked by visitors. When we arrived I had never seen the area filled with as much colour as that day. The warm sun had transformed the grass and sprinkled it with a rainbow of wildflowers.

"Oh Freddy, it's like a fairy tale here. Can we stay forever?"

"Anything for you, my Celia."

Over the next few weeks, I arranged for payment to be sent to Celia's Employer as compensation and stole her away in my little cottage. My parents were none the wiser, as I had used the money they set aside for me.

Every month, as promised, I would arrive around midday to spend time with my parents before they locked me away in that cellar, where my curse would be free to transform me safely. I never told Celia of my curse and hoped that for now we could just enjoy each other's company. To the outside world, Celia was my housekeeper, but inside the house we were happy and as one. I often wondered why loving someone was wrong—surely you love whoever you love—if only society could see how much we loved each other.

Then came a time in our lives when a disease spread throughout the lands. People stopped visiting our woods and meadows, and I soon received word that my parents had become ill and that I was advised not to attend. My parents were the only ones who knew about my secret and now the refuge they had offered me for so many years had been taken away. We were safe in our cottage, away from all of the death and disease, but it left me with only two days to plan what I was to do with myself, when my curse was upon me. I not only had to ensure Celia's safety, but also everyone that was in reach of my nightly wanderings. I had no idea what distance my wolf side could manage in a night. I had no cellar and no chains to secure me down. All I could rely on was the woods and the surrounding area. Maybe, I thought, if I found a nice cattle field miles from home, then I would be satisfied with devouring a few dozen cows. It was the only choice I had.

I explained to Celia that I was going to take a trip out to hunt for pheasant and I set off the day before with my bow and arrow, rope and a few other provisions. I kissed her lips and left her in the house, alone.

I walked for what seemed like forever, I did not stop for a break nor for food. I ate and sipped water while I walked, refilling it in rivers and streams, as I continued on. I tried my hardest to keep as much distance as I could from the towns, and just as the sun set, I found a field filled with sheep and climbed a tall tree, as high as I could safely go, and tied myself down. I could hear the sheep bleating as the sun disappeared under the horizon. As I looked around, I could just about see the farmer's dwelling far in the distance. A light was gently glowing in the upstairs window, as the occupant went to bed. The sheep in the field below me all seemed to drop where they stood, resembling white rocks that twitched from time to time. I willed the farmer to extinguish his light to keep my thirst from his house, but most of all, I prayed to every god that I could think of, to protect my Celia from my curse.

This night, the skies were completely clear and the stars shone with their brilliance. I watched as the horizon brightened, announcing the coming of my deadly foe. I glanced over to the farmhouse and was relieved to see that the light had indeed been extinguished. I tried my hardest to put the house as far from my thoughts as I could. I opened my eyes wide as the first beams of light burst across the furthest field, bringing with it the racing thoughts of my Celia. My spine began to ache, but I refused to close my eyes. My heart galloped like a herd of wild horses, my chest felt tight as my lungs had trouble keeping my blood oxygenated. I felt the immense torture of overwhelming tiredness. I shouted loudly into the night to keep myself conscious. Fingers ached as dagger-like claws pierced the skin under my nails and I used them to claw at my own flesh. I had to stay awake, sleeping would mean that all hope would be lost. I yelled out as loud as I could and as I did, my scream transformed into the howl of my wolf curse.

The sheep all rolled onto their feet and bolted across the field. I tried to give chase but I had tied myself down and fell, dangling by my legs from the branch. I threw up my wire-haired arm and swiped at the rope, slicing it like it was merely a web from a spider. As I fell, my body twisted and I landed on all four limbs. My jaw had protruded to extraordinary lengths and my sense of smell was phenomenal. I could smell everything, including the last wisps of smoke that still lingered in the air from the farmer's candle. Instinct took over my body and I began racing in the direction of the farm house. This time I had managed to keep myself awake and appeared to have a certain amount of restraint.

"No," I said to myself. "No humans. Look at those sheep, nice juicy mutton."

I tried to imagine the warm flesh dripping from my teeth, the taste of lamb, so delicious. It seemed to work for a while. The wolf in me seemed to enjoy darting around the field trying to catch those bundles of wool, and I did indeed tear out the throats of half a dozen at least. But the flesh was not so tasty and the woolly coats felt rough to swallow. The farmhouse was back

171

in my sights. The farmer and maybe his plump wife tucked up in bed. Nice warm flesh, hairless and red; meat eaters flesh, not grass-fed fodder. I tried to stop myself but it was impossible. The wolf was fast and was invading my brain, trying to send me to sleep. It was becoming tired of my demands. I decided that if I was to save one person, then I would save all my energy and fight for her. I would have to remain quiet while the wolf did what he had to do. When we reached the house, I could smell the dung-covered boots by the front door, but I could also smell the fresh meat hung up in the barn to bleed. It was a smell that was like honey on fresh bread; so tempting, so delicious. In an instant the barn door splintered into a thousand pieces and the meat slid down my throat. Surely that would satisfy the wolf. Surely.

Time skipped and before I was aware of anything else, we were leaping through the fields. I had caught hold of a scent, the scent that my body had made the day before. I had left a trail that the wolf was following and my heart filled with fear for my darling Celia.

"No," I demanded. "Don't you touch her. Don't you dare."

With all my might, I dug my claws into the ground and turned my body to face the other direction. I looked around for other opportunities but I was in the middle of nowhere. All I had was the scent and my wolf knew that it would lead to a meal. I felt powerless, I could only pray that the moon would hide away. Faster and faster the wolf sprinted through the countryside, locked on my scent. I could barely see our surroundings flashing past my eyes.

Then the wolf stopped. I felt a fear course through my body. Something was here. My spine pushed up the hairs on my back and I began to growl. I was at the witch tree and something about it gave me the shivers. The tree glowed with a blue haze and shimmered in the moonlight. I looked up at the face in the bark and crouched low to the ground, my gaze never leaving the face while I slowly crept past. I thought that by some miracle, the witch in the tree would spring to life and stop my wolf in its tracks, maybe even free me of my curse with her magic. At that moment I even wished for her to end my life to save my sweet Celia. Tonight this was not to be. As the tree fell behind me, my legs began racing once more and in what felt like no time, I was staring at my cottage. I begged and cried for mercy, promised my wolf anyone else in the world, just not her. Please not her.

I closed my eyes. I could not face bearing witness to my sweetheart's murder by my own bite. I gave in to sleep as the wolf leapt over the wall.

I woke up on the front lawn of my parents' home surrounded by both of their

173

corpses and their staff, two horses and two police officers. I was completely naked, shivering and covered with blood and flesh. I cannot bear to think of what the wolf did to my sweet Celia. I haven't asked as I fear what they might tell me.

At noon, I am to face the gallows and I have requested that after my death, my head must be detached and buried at least a mile from my body to prevent the wolf from returning.

I like to keep it in mind that my Celia still lives. That in the end, my love for her made my wolf form see how powerful our love was, and let her be.

FREDDY

Dear Freddy,

If only you knew that I went to your place in the woods and took the path you described. There I found a brown lady sitting on your bench reading a book, a beauty in your eyes I'm sure. She was very much alive and was waiting for you to return. I had the ghastly task in informing her of your demise. She wept instantly and told me of the deep love you felt for one another. I asked her about the night of your story. She did indeed have a visitation from a wolf that night, but explained that the beast seemed docile so she thought it to be a lost pet dog. She gave it food and water but as she passed the wolf some meat, it bit her hand. It wasn't a bad bite, only a nip, but it broke the skin. When I saw the scar, it had miraculously healed after only a week. So it seems that you can rest in peace knowing that she is alive and well.

Your friend, Peter

FOREVER WILD
Esme Knight & Diane Narraway

The howl rose like the full moon. It echoed above the canopy of the forest and bounced off the surrounding mountains. Below, shrouded in the darkness, a silhouette slipped through the trees, silent and unseen. The hooded figure stopped for a moment inclining their head towards the sound. It could not be far now. The ragged cliff face, and dense woodland made it difficult to judge; their prey could be higher up on the mountainside and to climb the steep face would be impossible at night, even in the moonlight. They continued to stalk through the wood, hoping that the beast would be closer to the ground. Returning empty-handed was not an option, there was more than just a matter of pride at stake; perhaps even a life hung in the balance. Her life.

Stories had always been told of how bold young women were tempted and enticed away into the woods during the harvest full moon, as if a blood-tithe must be paid for the bounty reaped. Nobody ever explained what had tempted them, it was simply referred to as the Howling. Over time, the Howling had become little more than an excuse for the Elders to send those they viewed as feisty or troublesome, or simply those they did not care for, into the wood as punishment.

Punishment for what, wasn't always clear, but nonetheless, they sent at least one girl every year. Some returned cowed, eyes never leaving the ground, and were quickly married. Some returned with an inner madness and were cast out beyond the edge of the village, to remain spinsters until their final breath. Some did not return at all.

They could call it what they liked, it was the women that intrigued the Hunter; more specifically those who did not return. Where did they go? Were they captured? Enslaved? Eaten? And if so, by what? Was the beast just a fairy story to scare little girls into what they believed was 'nice behaviour'? Maybe originally it had been to warn them of the dangers that could befall a little girl lost in the forest. Or was there perhaps a kernel of truth in it somewhere? Or did these poor girls just run away to find a better life? One less judged perhaps. These questioned burned in her mind, and having been the one sent into the forest, she was hell bent on finding answers.

Her thoughts were interrupted by the howl rising into the night. She sighed. She had already spent one night in the forest listening to that howl being carried on the breeze, and all the while getting further away. The Hunter kept hoping that it was another answering the call and not that her prey was, as she feared, becoming more distant. This was her last chance to not only slay the beast, if there was indeed a beast to slay, but to find answers to the burning questions that had led her to the forest in the first place.

The moon was just reaching its apex, which at this time of year meant that there were only a couple of hours left before dawn, and once the soft light began to filter through the forest her chance would be gone. She would have to wait until the evening to pick up the trail again. Local folklore told how the beast only came out during the full moon and left no trace, not even after three nights. It was as if it was supernatural—a ghost. It was already the second night of the full moon's three-day cycle and the Hunter had made good ground. She would neither waste the moonlight, nor would she return cowed, branded mad, or become enslaved. The fabled beast that cursed the women of the village would be revealed and defeated once and for all. She would return with its head for all to see. It would be proof that her wild nature and rebellious behaviour were gifts that could benefit all, as opposed to something that needed to be cured or punished.

Another hour passed before the she felt the first prickle through her body that something was amiss. The wind brought a sour tang with it and the wood did not feel as empty as it had done earlier. She was fully aware that she was now the one being hunted and that she

179

would have to think quickly in order to not give herself away. She continued following the trail, but more cautiously, heading towards a safer place on higher ground. This, she hoped, would not only protect her, but perhaps give her a better view of both her hunter and her prey.

Moving slowly and purposefully, the Hunter continued following the trail, dipping to the ground every thirty paces or so to check for markers: paw prints, droppings, scraps of fur, food or anything else. She knew it was a risky call, but she hoped it would buy her a little more time in order to work out who was stalking her. She headed for the Tor; a rocky outcrop of giant boulders tumbled into a pile by an ancient glacier, as if they were marbles. There she could find small, but high up places where she could hide. Taking a steady breath and dropping to a crouch, the Hunter bowed her head and closed her eyes, allowing her other senses to heighten. The dank odour resembled moss on a cave wall, mingled with a sickly musk, she felt the dry panting and heard the soft crunch of leaves underfoot. Or more precisely, under feet! She worked out there were at least three hounds that were less than a hundred yards away, and judging by the lack of human voices, they were unleashed, and master-less. The Hunter needed to be close enough to the Tor to outrun them in less time than it would take for the pack to catch her up; her heartbeat quickened at the thought.

Whether the dogs heard her heart pounding, or whether they smelt the fear was hard to determine, but the long low growl, that rumbled through her ribcage told her time was of the essence.

She grasped the hem of her cloak, pulling it high enough so as not to trip, and taking a firm grip on the handle of her sword, the Hunter shifted her weight ready to sprint. Another growl rolled out from the shadow; the hounds were gaining ground. It had to be now, otherwise the hounds would flank and close in. She closed her eyes, took a deep breath and swallowed hard, before opening them and running for all she was worth. She was nimble and surefooted over the uneven floor of the forest, leaping ditches and vaulting fallen branches. She knew this place, it was her sanctuary: every bank, every dyke, every fallen oak, and every stream. The Elders had always said spending too much time in the wood was unnatural, that it would lead to an inner wildness and in turn forsake the protection of the village. The Hunter did not care. The forest was sacred, it was alive; the wind whispered to her through the trees, while the stream's beautiful song captivated her, lifting her spirit when she was down, and the rocky tor offered shelter when needed. The forest offered its own protection to those who loved it. If there was a supernatural beast that prowled it each full moon; sometimes wolf, sometimes human, that so callously broke and shamed so many of her sisterhood, then she would find it and bring its reign of terror to an end by delivering the beast's head, while wearing its still bloody pelt.

The Hunter's concentration faltered as her mind wandered to her glorious victory, briefly forgetting the slavering dogs that were growing ever closer. She lost her footing, slipping on the rotting mulch and tumbled into a heap; her bow slid off her shoulder and her quiver spilled arrows that were to be lost among the bracken. The Tor, if it wasn't, certainly seemed a fair distance away and the shadows of the hounds were now visible among the trees.

"Get up ... Get up!" she willed herself, still slightly winded from the fall, stumbling a little as she stooped to grab her fallen weapons, before racing off once more into the night. Her hood fell backwards, revealing a mass of unruly locks and fierce eyes. The silvery light of the full moon touched her skin, illuminating the hounds' quarry, and the hunt quickened as she aimed for the Tor, running as fast as she could.

With her fist full of arrows and her cloak billowing behind her, she ducked through the low branches and into a clearing. The full moon drenched the majestic form of the Tor, stacked clumsily under the cold clear sky in front of her in silvery light. The copse was dense at the foot of the rock, but she knew the path and she hoped the hounds didn't. She didn't even break step as she hopped up onto the stone.

The pack of dogs, their jaws slack with saliva, burst through the tree line. She risked a glance over her shoulder to see them grind to a halt trying to navigate the dense thorny bushes; she could hear their hunger and she knew it wouldn't be long before they would break through the undergrowth and resume their chase. She was right. Moments later they were only feet away. They slowed and fanned out to flank her on either side. She kept going, each stride steeper and higher, as they followed her, first onto the low stones that poked through the earth, gaining distance as they climbed. The contrast of the hard, stone surface compared to the soft forest floor was an immediate advantage to the hounds and before long they were snapping at her heels. But still she climbed.

She could hear the howl of her prey in the distance, but knew that she had no chance of resuming her hunt, not now, not while she herself was being hunted.

A hound caught the corner of her cloak in its sharp teeth and shook its head vigorously, leaning back on its haunches, tugging at her, determined to pull her from the rock. She could see the bloodlust in its eyes. It was a look she knew well. She had seen it in her own eyes only the night before. She slipped slightly, just managing to kick out, connecting the toe of her boot squarely on its jaw. Whimpering, it rolled away, threads of fabric still lacing its mouth. Using the momentum of the kick she tried desperately to swing herself up onto a ledge out of their reach, but to no avail. She slipped slightly and came face to face with the hounds. She gripped her sword tighter than ever, determined not to be their prey and a fleeting thought passed through her mind; Could this have been the fate of those before her?

She heard the howl of the wolf she had been stalking. He seemed closer now, but so many thoughts were racing through her head that it was impossible to really be sure of anything. She was determined to stand her ground, however futile; she would not go down without a fight! Thrashing at the hounds with her sword, the howl which had been growing ever closer was now clearly visible.

He was her size, if not larger, and she was petrified. His large canines glinted in the moonlight as they dripped saliva onto the cold ground before her. She froze, unable to move. It became apparent that she had grossly underestimated her prey, as she witnessed the fury that followed as wolf and hounds fought only inches away from her. The fierce clashing of teeth and claws seemed to go on forever, and though she was unharmed, she was unsure of the best course of action; to run or remain as still as she could. She chose the latter. Eventually, the injured hounds fled, whimpering into the night and the wolf lay bleeding at her feet.

Now was her chance. She could either leave the villagers' demon wolf for dead, or finish him and return triumphant as had been the original plan. Her heart was still pounding with fear, and adrenaline surged through her as she tentatively edged close enough to look into his eyes, hoping to see the menacing evil that had terrorised so many before her, but instead, the moonlight revealed what appeared to be tears. She ventured nearer, captivated by the unending depth, she stared into the abyss. The Hunter sensed within him the same wild spirit that lived within her, and as his eyes burned deep into her soul, she knew that there was no hiding her true nature, and that he was fully aware it had been him that she was stalking through the forest.

But now as he lay helpless, she felt no hatred towards him, and no longer wondered about him, instead her curiosity was piqued, and different thoughts now raced through her mind. Was the wolf, and for that matter, was she, not so much cursed but blessed with a freedom of spirit beyond the villagers' comprehension? And what of those who had gone before her?

What did they, or didn't they, know? What were they afraid of? Had they too been chased by hounds? And had they taken the time to discover the wolf's inner beauty? Hell!

185

Did they even see the wolf? Or were they simply afraid of what lay in the forest? Or maybe they were just afraid of their own true natures. And the most compelling question of all ... Where was the wolf the rest of the month? Or even, come the break of day?

She wouldn't have long to find out as there were only a couple of hours left till daybreak. She had no wish to injure this creature, she wanted only to help him, after all he had saved her from the hounds, and it was as if she could hear the voice of his heart whispering to her.

She lit a fire, partially to keep warm—the night, short as it was, had developed a chill in the air—but mostly to keep the hounds away; fire can be an excellent weapon. She tended his wounds as best she could and shared what little food she had, and in return she felt his companionship. Eventually, with only an hour till daybreak, she curled up beside the wolf. The warmth from his body felt good and although she desperately wanted to stay awake, within minutes she was asleep.

She had no idea how long she slept for, but she awoke to a new sense of loneliness. She knew he would return tonight, and this time she would discover, once and for all, the mystery that surrounded both him and the annual Howling. She would search all night for the wolf if she had to, not as Hunter and prey, but as kindred spirits.

As the third night drew closer, she knew that returning to the village was not an option— not now, not ever! Shades of red and orange blazed across the sky as the sun set on the third and final night, silhouetting the forest as darkness grew ever closer.

The wind gently rustled through the trees and she caught the first faint hint of his scent. She knew he was close by and for the first time she felt safe. As his scent grew stronger, excitement surged up through her body and she felt the howl rise from deep within. She knew she would be forever wild!

Based on an original song, written and performed by Esme Knight, and featured as a duet with Martin Jackson on the Forever Wild album (Produced by Josh Elliott (JGE Studios)).

IT WAS TIME
Marisha Kiddle

I threw my last item of clothing on the ground and looked at him. My mate, my love, my life, my alpha.

We had played out this scene many times over the years, but tonight something was different. Something was off. I could smell it in the air—on him, on me—it was everywhere. The awareness that someone was watching us was so strong, it caused the hairs on the back of my neck to rise up in warning.

The moon peeked over the top of the hill before us, daring us to greet her.

He looked at me. I shivered.

It was time.

My mouth watered in anticipation of what lay ahead of us. He took my hands and kissed my head as he had done many times before.

It began.

The heat burned through my body, emanating from where he'd kissed me through to the bottom of my naked feet in the cool, damp grass. The intense pain of the change soared through every bone, muscle, and sinew.

It was time.

He nuzzled his lupine nose into my neck and nipped at me, encouraging me to start, to make that first move—challenging me to prove my worthiness as his mate, his lover.

We walked side by side towards the hill. Our hill, where we had met and where he had made me his mate. His dominance gave him an air of grace and dignity, something nobody else could ever achieve in my eyes. He nudged me again, bringing me back to my senses. I picked up the scent of an intruder, but he didn't turn, or look, or smell the air. It didn't bother him. Was it safe?

Our pace increased. We gathered speed, him nudging and challenging me to go faster, to race, to run. He led and I followed. The scent got stronger, the intruder came closer, and my mind whirled, but I didn't look back for fear of stumbling or losing my pace.

Then she was there, level with me, neck and neck. I could feel my strength waning in her presence. Had he known she would come? Had he encouraged this stranger to try and take my place?

I had to keep up. I had to beat her. I had to keep my mate.

She was younger, more beautiful, and fitter than me. She pulled a nose length ahead of me. Nobody had ever beaten me, in all the years that I had raced. I'd been challenged twice before, and I had always been the fittest.

I felt the wind blow across my fur as she began to pass me; my heart lurched to my stomach, and for the first time I faltered.

She passed me fully and I weakened further; I wasn't even halfway up the hill by the time she was almost at the top.

I fell.

Laying in the damp grass I looked up and saw them howling to the sky while the full moon cast them in silhouette. She had won. She had taken my place as the alpha's mate. My heart slowed; my time approaching its end. I was broken.

I looked once more as they shifted back into their naked human forms. He lifted her chin and kissed her lovingly. I had grown too old for him. He had indeed encouraged her to race me.

It was time.

I closed my eyes and plunged into the eternal sleep.

PAT-A-CAKE, PAT-A-CAKE.
Jack Callaghan.

"Look at him," said Henry, staring at the screen with utter contempt, "dancin' up and down. What's he supposed to be?"

Even so many years after its initial popularity, Michael Jackson's 'Thriller' is still played on most music TV channels, with astonishing regularity.

"I don't think he's supposed to be owt, is he?" asked Don as he watched Jackson gyrating at the head of his dancing horde of whatever they were supposed to be. "He's just ... a monster."

"No, watch how it goes, from start to end," said Henry, waving his half full pint glass at the screen. "First, he's a werewolf, then he's a zombie, then he's a werewolf again. He wants to take his fuckin' pick. Offensive, is what it is. He may as well be wearing black-face."

"He was black, wasn't he?" asked Don.

"That's not the point," said Henry. "Unfair representation, that's the point. Jacko got the idea for this video after he saw that American werewolf in London film." He gave a snort of derision. "I'll tell you what an American werewolf in London would get. Mugged and stabbed up by yobbos with Stanley blades, that's what."

"Silver Stanley blades?" asked Don. He wasn't having any of it. He'd heard this routine from Henry more times that he could count. "You've got to remember; this was all before. Back before it all came out. They only had stuff like films to go with."

"Bollocks!" Henry spat. "We've been around for thousands of years, but they suddenly go all daft and bozz-brained, because the younger ones can't keep their fuckin' mouths shut."

"Better to be all out and in the open, though. Right?" said Don. "No more lurking in the shadows."

"Again, bollocks!" said Henry. "I don't even know why I'm talking to you. You're one of them. Don't you forget, mate. I was born a werewolf. I wasn't turned into one, like you. I am of the original, ancient, noble bloodline of the Lupercal, descended from Romulus and Remus themselves!"

"And now living in Lancashire," said Don with a snigger. "Ancient and noble indeed."

"I'll wipe that grin off of your clock in a minute," said Henry. "What're you gonna do if Black-Shirt Billy wins the next election, and they start forcing you to do what they want?"

William Godwin-Smyth—Black-Shirt Billy—had started off as a member of a relatively fringe political group, until he was one of the first to declare that his party would provide, 'A definitive answer to the ever-growing

Lycanthropus issue'. He used the Latin word 'Lycanthropus', because it sounded less like 'Werewolf', and he used the term 'Definitive answer', because it sounded less like 'Final solution'.

"Twelve days in a year locked up," said Don with a shrug. "I can think of worse. I don't remember owt of what happens every full. Do you? They put you in the room, the full comes, you tear-arse around like a dick-head for a bit, and then you wake up the next day like nothing had ever happened. It could work."

"How many people have you killed in the last year?" asked Henry, narrowing an eye at Don.

"None," said Don, again giving a shrug. "I've got it all sorted. I get one of my mates to strap me to the bed with these proper, unbreakable leather and buckle things. These folks from an S&M club helped me out. I get black-out drunk as well. Honestly, it helps. You come around, all raging and snarling, but your body's still too sauced to do anything. Smack does it, too, they tell me, but I'm not going near that. It gets too many of us. Not all Smack-heads are werewolves, but a lot of werewolves are Smack-heads." He narrowed his own eye at Henry. "Why? How many have you killed?"

"No humans," said Henry with a shake of his head. "What I do is go up into the hills and find a field with a good-sized flock of sheep or herd of cattle. Fifty for sheep usually does it,

195

ten to twenty for cows. I lay myself down in a bush before nightfall. The full comes, I spend all night ripping my way through the beasts, and I just have to hope that I come around before the farmer finds me the next day. Honestly, beef steaks, lamb shanks, I can't even look at them during the rest of the month. I'm a vegetarian, you know."

"What's your point?" asked Don.

"My point," said Henry, "is that, unlike us, there are plenty who don't do anything to prepare for the full at all. They just let it fly. That's why you hear about, 'So-and-so dead. No suspects', or, 'Went mad and killed all of his kids. No motive'. 'Spontaneous Family Annihilators' they call them in The States." He tapped his finger on the table. "Chris Watts. He was one of us. I'll bet you anything."

"Again," said Don, "what's your point?"

"Let's put it like this," said Henry, rolling his head from side to side across his shoulders. "In America, towards the start of the century, they tried this thing called 'Prohibition'. Too many people drinking, you see. So, what they did was they made alcohol illegal. But, making alcohol illegal doesn't rid the world of alcoholics. All it does is make alcoholics criminals, while also penalising those who enjoy alcohol responsibly. Ergo, everyone suffers."

"This isn't quite the same as that," said Don, waving for the barman.

"Isn't it?" asked Henry. "You live in a world where alcohol exists, the guy next-door to you gets plastered every night, beats his wife, neglects his kids, while you fancy the odd glass of wine every now and then. But, no. You're not allowed to. Because, you, too, may one day drink too much. You cannot be trusted. What if your fancy S&M straps break? What if you forget? The full doesn't happen once every calendar month. Oh, no. The lunar cycle shifts. It actually happens every twenty-nine and half days. If you do agree to go into voluntary confinement, who shall it be who'll decide the length of it? Sometimes there are more than 12 fulls in a year. Also, are we talking day or night? Sometimes, you see the moon and the sun in the sky at the same time. What even is a full moon? We know it's nothing to do with light. Photons that reflect off of the moon are the same photons that come from the sun. So, is it to do with gravity, maybe? The moon makes the tides go in and out. So, does that maybe do something to us? Something to do with the liquids of our flesh, perhaps? Does the full moon draw the wretched vapours of some of the species Homo-Erectus to the point where they transmogrify altogether? No, of course not. All we know is that it does, we don't know how, and we don't know why, but it does. The only reason that we were dragged out of the fog of superstition and folklore is because there are now too many of us. We live in a world of mobile

197

phones, of video calls and live-streaming. If there was such thing as ghosts, Big-foot, or UFOs, some bugger would've recorded one by now. The reason that the Lycanthrope race was made public knowledge is, as you well know, due to the Morris video."

The Morris video, or 'Oor bairn is fookin wyrd!' was the first genuine documented footage of a Lycanthropic transformation. At first it was dismissed as trickery, though many of those involved in cinematic special effects were quoted as saying, 'It must, of course, be fake, but we don't know how they're doing it'.

The sprouting of hair and the elongation of the skull were what left most observers perplexed. Though, as the video grew in popularity, the conclusion was obvious; bring the child in front of proper cameras, and let's see this for ourselves. The parents refused, not wishing to be drawn into the maelstrom of reality television. However, calls, letters and emails began to pour in. Not lots, but enough, saying something akin to, 'My baby does the same', 'Our baby sprouts and sheds hair like a barber shop', 'Our baby has claws and can climb up onto the ceiling', 'Our baby ate our cockapoo', and so on.

All of this was, again, dismissed, until Constance Morris, the baby herself, was fifteen years old and allowed to speak her mind. At first, she was distraught, thinking she was the only person in the world to suffer from these ailments, that no-one else seemed to believe in. That is, apart from a very few, very specific people in the darkest corners of the internet, 'Come on, sweetie, chew my knot', but she refused to have anything to do with them.

As more and more people came forward, the ridicule, and then the disbelief, began to diminish. People who had, for their entire lives, been burdened by their true nature, began to come forward. Not only in Britain, but all over the world. The initial response was simple; these people are making it up. Murderers, psychopaths, anyone looking for any excuse. Let's see you turn into a wolf! And then, they did. At the age of twenty-one, Constance Morris married a man from Luxembourg and gave birth to the first, internationally recognised Lycanthrope. This also brought to public attention the fact that Lycanthropes go through a period of homicidal rage during full moons, when Constance and her new fledgling family transformed, on camera, and then proceeded to kill, disembowel, and then partially eat the entire film crew, before fleeing to who only knows where.

'Something must be done!' media outlets soon demanded. 'How many more are at large throughout the country?'

'It's a landslide! William Godwin-Smyth is elected Prime Minister!'

Don shouldered his bag as the van drew up. It stopped right in front of his house, and two men got out, leaving the engine to idle.

"Name?" the foremost of them asked, before he was even halfway across the road.

"What?" asked Don.

"Name!" the second man said, much more forcefully. "Answer me, dog boy!"

"Perkins," said Don. "Donald Perkins. What ..."

"Leave the bag," the first of the men said. "You won't need it."

"But it's got my ..."

"I said you won't need it. You're only going to be held for two days. Everything you need will be provided for you."

"Oh, okay," said Don. "I'll put it back inside."

"Leave it where it is," the first man said. "Leave it where it is and step away from it."

"I'll just take out a few things," said Don, thinking he'd at least need a toothbrush, a comb, maybe some deodorant.

"I said step away from it!" the second man growled. He raised his arm and held it out at a right angle to his body. The sleeve of his jacket went right to his wrist, but, from the cuff of it, there suddenly sprang three, foot-long tendrils of wiry metal. They twisted and undulated in front of his palm, as though they had a mind of their own. Each twitching wire hissed and popped as a strange, incandescent

200

liquid began to flow along it. "You know what this is?" the bearer asked, and Don only nodded, his head lowered.

Formally, this dreadful thing was called a 'Temporary Incapacitant Device', but it was more commonly known as a 'Dog leash'. Within an instant, the officer in front of Don could whip his arm around, and the three tendrils would shoot out, ranging up to fifteen feet, and wrap around him, their barbed points going for his mouth, his nose, his eyes, all the time pumping an agony-inducing cocktail of nerve toxin.

Don had never seen one in action, but he'd heard about them from a guy called 'Hombre-Lobo', The Bat-Shit-Mexican. "Hurts like a sun-ov-a-beech, Ese," he'd said. Lobo had been forced to have his entire right leg amputated after only a few seconds of contact with the dreaded 'Dog leash', so Don was taking no chances.

"Leave the bag," the dog leash wielder said, "or I'll fuckin' sting you."

"Okay," said Don, raising his hands up in surrender.

"All the same," the second man said. "See how they bend. You think you can go around chewing people up, but see how you shake when we threaten to put the pain on you. 'Shaking like a shitting dog', as they say."

"What?" Don asked again. It was the only word he could think of.

"What? What? What?" his tormenter parroted. "You not got anything new? Leave the bag, get in the van. Why are we drawing this out? You fuckin' people disgust me. Get in the van!"

Don obeyed and, leaving his bag, went around to the broad door of the van. The first man opened it just enough for Don to squeeze inside, and he was met with a row of benches across each side of the vehicle. One was occupied by a single man, the other by a woman and a small girl, with just enough room for Don to sit beside them.

As Don shifted in next to the girl, trying to gather his thoughts, she suddenly began to sing.

"Pat-a-cake, pat-a-cake, baker's man", she sang, clapping her hands together in a one-two-three rhythm. "Pat-a-cake, pat-a-cake, pat-a-cake."

"She's been at it since I got in," the man across from Don said with a shake of his head. He raised a hand and tapped his temple. "Lost it, poor mite."

"Pat-a-cake, pat-a-cake ..."

"Where are they taking us?"

"Pat-a-cake ..."

"Somewhere down South. It's where they've been rounding us up."

"... baker's man. Pat-a-cake ..."

"Rounding up? What do you mean? It's just for two days."

"... Pat-a-cake, pat-a-cake, baker's man."

"Could you stop that, sweetheart? Just for one moment. What do you mean, rounding up?"

"Some big place down South. You go there, or they fuck your whole family over. That's what I was told. You, and anyone else, identify yourself as a werewolf and go voluntarily, or they take you all by force."

"They can't do that!"

"... baker's man ..."

"Look at where you are, mate. They just did. Black-Shirt Billy runs the show now, and he does whatever he wants."

"Black-Shirt Billy, baker's-man ..."

"Can you shut her up, please?" asked Don, levelling a finger at the small girl's mother. "I'm trying to think!"

"Nothing shuts her up," the mother replied. "She can go at it for hours. Though, I must say, this is the longest so far."

"It's giving me a headache," said Don as the engine of the van rumbled into life.

"It's giving us all a headache," said the man seated across from Don. "Just zone it out."

"It's not just a headache, though," said Don, wincing and screwing his eyes shut. "It's like a needle in my brain. Seriously, sweetie. Can you stop that?"

"No," the girl said, suddenly breaking from her mantra for the first time so far, and looking Don right in the eye. "I won't stop. You're just not listening."

"Crikey!" said her mother. "I've not heard her say that before. You should listen up, mate."

"It's almost the full," the girl said, a strange and almost dreamy look in her eyes as she looked at Don. "That's why they've gathered us together. Are you ready?"

"What?" asked Don. This was his word of the day.

"The full is coming," the girl said. "I feel it. They got us too late. Hold my hand."

Don reached out and took hold of her hand, even though he knew she was wrong. How could they even guess if the full was happening from inside the confines of the van?

"Wait a moment," said the man across from Don. "Do you feel that? Ow! My calves! It always gets me in my calves! They stretch, and ... Argh! God!"

Don looked down and, indeed, the man's legs were moving, just not in a natural way, he shifted and twisted them in the small space that the van would allow. He dragged each leg out in front of him and rubbed at them. The right, then the left leg extended from the knee, elongating over three feet, the flesh of his leg emerging from the cuff of his trousers, the stitching at the knee bulging from the growth.

As he watched this, Don suddenly felt similar changes start up within himself. The

204

ache in the back teeth, the tensing of the shoulders, the pressure building within the brow, as though the skull was fit to burst, the widening and cracking of the sternum as it spread outwards and upwards. The arching of the spine. The widening of the hips.

Don looked back into the young girl's face. She had changed also. It wasn't quite complete, but it was near enough. It was now that he understood that the full was only part of the spell. What was needed to make it complete was this connection, the holding of hands, the coming together of two, three, now four other Lycanthropes, as he saw that the girl's mother and the other passenger were now also joined in a hand-hold. This was what was needed to truly channel the power of the full.

Not only was it happening faster than usual, and apparently far too early, but Don was astonished to find that the dreaded red mist of the change had failed to descend. The white-hot second of rage that preceded the black-out—Don had often described it as being similar to the pop of bright light that came from being hit in the face—had not come, nor had the resulting unconsciousness. Instead, and even though the transformation was well underway, Don found that he was still completely in his right mind.

He felt his face changing. His teeth grew, his jaw jutted out. He felt his back snap as his vertebrae shifted. The others were also

205

changing. Here a claw, there a sharpened fang or double-jointed forearm.

As Don's fingers snapped and cracked into seven-inch talons, he looked back at the small girl, her features now transformed into a lupine rictus of pure malice. She looked towards the front of the van.

"Kill them!" she said, her voice now robbed of its previous delicacy and turned into a savage deadpan growl, without emotion or inflection. "Kill them all!"

"Will you shut your fuckin' gobs!" came a voice from the driver's cab. "Sat back there, chiming on like God knows what. You'll be pissing your pants when you see where we're takin' you!"

Don wound his hand up, tensed his forearm, and sunk it right through the sheet of metal between the rear of the van and the front seats with every ounce of strength that he had.

The driver looked down at the fist and two feet of forearm sticking out of his chest, erupting in a flower of gore.

"Hey," he said. "That's not meant to be there."

As he collapsed backwards, Don pushed his intruding hand further through him and took hold of the wheel. He spun it hard to the right, intending to turn the whole vehicle over, but the other passenger, that Don had completely forgotten about, seized the wheel and wrenched it the other way, causing the van to come to a juddering halt, but the sudden jack-knife was more than the top-heavy vehicle could manage, and it rocked up onto one side, all those within falling into each other as it lurched sideways, the rightmost wheels leaving the ground.

Don darted for the sliding side door. His hands, still coated in the driver's innards, made easy work of the lock and he swiftly threw it open, letting the girl, her mum, and the third fellow jump down onto the road.

The surviving man in the passenger seat also leaped out, narrowly missing a crushing as the van collapsed onto its side.

"You fuckin' villains!" he spat at them as he scrambled to his feet. "Trouble causing, van wrecking, doggo fuckers! I'll have you all skinned alive! I'll ..." It was only now that he laid eyes upon his captives in their transformed state. His face fell when he saw the rows of fangs, the bristles, the claws. "Alright," he said. "Let's not do anything hasty."

The little girl took one, very purposeful step towards him.

"You," he said as she looked right at him, her eyes like drill-bits. "Little sweetness. Didn't I give you that peach earlier? I'm alright, aren't I? I was only doing what I was told. We were just taking you somewhere safe. It was for your own good!"

His head then exploded, coating everything around him in a sheen of bright, vermillion blood, skull fragments and brain matter.

"Oi!" the girl's mum said, wiping the blood from the font of her jumper. "You never told me he gave you a peach. And, you never told me that you could do a head pop! I'll be watching you!"

Don wiped the blood from his face, it'd given him a good splattering, and said, "First thing I need to do is go back home and tell Henry. My word will his face be ... " He looked down at his hand. "Well ... red. He only lives a few streets from here. I need to go and warn him."

"I'm afraid there's no going home now," the man who'd been sat across from Don said, wiping the dust from his clothes, even though they were now tattered and torn, due to his changing. His entire suit was ripped open, his newly elongated limbs poking out at acute angles. "They'll be on the look-out." He looked down at himself and gave a chuckle. "Strangest thing. I've never seen myself like this before. You hear horror stories about it, but now that I see it, it's not actually that bad. I could get used to this."

"How did you do this?" Don asked the girl. "And," he pointed to the decapitated body of the officer, "how did you do that?"

"Dunno," she said with a shrug of her shoulders. "Didn't know I could, until now. Not too weird, though. I can do all sorts of things. I just have to ..." She clapped her hands together. "Pat-a-cake, pat-a-cake."

"Baker's man, right," said Don. "Like you said."

"There's talk of a place up north," the mother said. "Somewhere everyone's gathering together, where Black-Shirt Billy can't reach. They say Constance Morris set it up, and she's still there, building an army, some say. Just trying to stay out of trouble sounds more like it."

"And, how do we get there?" asked Don.

"Should be easy," the mother said. "We just flag down a car, and ..." She shrugged, just as her daughter had done. "They take us where we want, or else we give 'em the old pat-a-cake."

"Well, if it's that easy," said Don with a smirk. "Okay. You lot get by the side of the road, and I'll stick my thumb out." He looked at his thumb. It was a seven-inch long, claw tipped, fur and gore covered thing right out of a nightmare. Surely, some good Samaritan of the road would have no problem pulling over for that.

THE GREATEST SHOW ON EARTH
Bekki Milner

Gerrent Brothers Circus
12th—16th August
Three nights only!

The Great Bandelerenos
Witness the most unbelievable sword
swallowing act of the century!

George Bandelereno twisted the end of his moustache and looked thoughtful. The lights framing the mirror reflected off his slicked back hair, and shimmered across the sequins of his white leotard. His partner, Gilda, spun around from her closet, her sequins dazzling him in the mirror.

"Can you believe they told us to move on?" she asked. "Horatio said there were twenty of them at least. All burly looking locals. Might as well have had pitchforks. Said we had no right, but it's been agreed with the council for months." Her graceful arms flapped as she pulled on her stockings. George had heard the commotion out by the big top earlier, and did what he always did—stayed out of it.

A number of locals had gathered and started shouting at the girl in the ticket booth. Shereen was only 19, but when confronted with a gang of angry men, she'd held her own until help had arrived in the form of Phillipe, the clown and unspoken ringmaster of Gerrent Brothers Circus. He was shortly followed by Andreas and Howard, two of the Russian acrobat troupe, and Mary, the lead dancer, who stood at over 6ft in her heels and feathers.

"I hear Phillipe and Mary saw them off well enough." George watched his wife in the mirror as she loaded the knives for their act into his belt. He wore it for their final trick; throwing the knives one by one as Gilda was turned round and round on a spinning board. It was one of the more daring tricks, and always gained a gasp from the audience.

"Let's hope they don't come back during the show." Gilda pouted, handing the belt to George, who fastened it about his hips. She leant the sabres that they both swallowed nightly by the door, and was reaching for her boots when something hit the side of the van with a bang, causing it to shake violently.

"What in the world—" George steadied himself and Gilda against the sudden force of movement, yanking up the blind at the window and peering outside for the cause of the tremors. A flash of dark fur—a large tail, he presumed—danced past the window before the van shook again. "That damn dog!" George cursed, and spun for the door. "I've warned Andreas to keep it under control!"

Goliath was a large but dim husky owned by the Russian tumbler. He was harmless, but clumsy, and often caused chaos when he got off the leash, sending popcorn stalls flying or tearing apart hay bales. George flung open the door, and jumped the steps to the grass, running round the front end of the van to confront the dog. Only, Goliath wasn't there.

The van was dented from the impact, nothing that couldn't be fixed, but frustrating none the less. But where was the dog?

The site hoarding panels that circled the camp were covered in large vinyl banners and locked into place, but there was a gap between the two panels right behind George's van where they had been pulled from their stays. He stuck his head between them, looking for the dog, and when he couldn't see him outside the camp, headed for Andreas' van.

A sharp rap on the door let George know that the husky was not missing; barking ensued from inside the van. Andreas opened the door to a bewildered and concerned George. If it wasn't Goliath, then another, unknown dog had hit his van and escaped through the fence.

Upon hearing the story, Andreas followed George back to his van, bringing Goliath with him. The husky stopped short of the back of the van, growling and sniffing the air. Something had been there that he clearly was not happy about, and Andreas had to grab his collar to stop him running away from the scent.

"Probably one of those farmers let his dog loose in the camp on purpose." Andreas shrugged, helping George repair the fence, "I'll ask around, see if anyone else saw something, but I wouldn't expect a big crowd tonight. By all accounts they're boycotting the circus."

Great, thought George. That meant they wouldn't get a full night's pay if the tickets hadn't sold. He ran his fingers over the dent in the wall of the van, wondering what size that dog had been to cause such damage.

"My love, we should head in." Glinda interrupted his thoughts, leaning through the window with a shower of glitter. The sun was setting, and the lights flickered on all around the camp. Music began to play from the big top—there wouldn't be guests for another hour at least, but it was time to go help set up for the evening.

Florence and Fabricio
Witness the most graceful and magical trapeze show in all of Europe!

Flying, floating, falling—Florence loved that brief fleeting moment when she let go of the trapeze and was suspended in mid-air, right before gravity took over and she fell into the safety net below.

214

Of course, there was no safety net during the show, but in the afternoons, when she practiced, she would end her hour by free-falling into the net, arms and legs outstretched and skirts around her ears as she lay there, waiting for it to stop vibrating. Fabricio would leave quietly, knowing just how much she enjoyed her post-practice nap in the net.

The lights that circled the big top were warm on her skin, chalk dust drifting through the beams, and the faint noise of people working, setting up stalls, practicing acts outside the big top was a gentle lullaby. She sighed with content, stretching her fingers and toes. Such familiar sounds and feelings were comforting.

Just as she drifted off, the air shifted and the sound of footsteps on the grass alerted her to the presence of someone in the big top. Sometimes, others passed through for whatever reason—needing to go backstage, fix a bench, change a lightbulb—but she didn't recognise these footsteps, or the masculine aftershave that drifted through the air.

Florence opened her eyes and sat up sharply, staring right at the perpetrator—a young man with broad shoulders, short dirty blonde hair, and startlingly bright blue eyes, wearing jeans and a grey, woollen jumper.

"Who are you? You're not supposed to be in here," she snapped; not appreciating her nap being disturbed.

The man raised his hands, palms towards her. "It's okay," he said. "I just need to tell you something."

He was nervous, his hands even shook a little. He had stopped walking towards her just inside the ring. He'd come from the backstage area, which meant he hadn't used the main entrance or passed the ticket booth.

"How did you get in here?" Florence gathered her skirts and backed towards the edge of the safety net, furthest away.

"Through the gate. It was open—look, I'm sorry. My names Peter." He let his hands drop, taking a couple of steps forward, and Florence in turn backed further to the rear of the net. She knew the stalls were behind her, and two rows of wooden steps that led to the foyer. She hoped that the stalls were still being built. She could scream, she supposed.

"Well, you're not meant to be here, Peter. Tickets are for sale out front." Florence grabbed the thick rope at the edge of the net with both hands behind her.

"I don't want tickets. But I need to ask you to leave. All of you, you need to go, tonight." Peter wrung his hands in front of him. "Please."

"Leave!?" Florence looked around for another sign of life. "We can't leave! We're booked to be here until tomorrow night. Three shows! Why would we leave?" Admittedly, ticket sales had been appalling, and there had been barely 30 people there from neighbouring

216

villages the night before. She'd heard about the gang of locals telling them to leave the day before. Was Peter one of them?

"Please, it's not safe, it's a full moon tomorrow and—"

"Peter!" A woman's voice interrupted from behind Florence, who spun round, barely hanging on to the net as it wobbled beneath her. A short brunette woman stood on the top step between the stalls, her arms crossed. "Peter, get home right now." She scowled, her face dark.

Peter hesitated, lowering his head. He seemed powerless as he crossed the ring towards the woman, who watched him mount the steps to the exit until he disappeared down the tented tunnel. She turned, her attention focused back on Florence.

"He's right. You should all leave." Her eyes glinted in the lights, her arms still firmly crossed over her chest. She shook her head, the brown curls falling around her shoulders. "The sooner the better."

With that, she turned on the wooden steps, her heels clicking as she followed Peter out. Florence realised she hadn't heard her enter and wondered how the woman knew Peter was even in here. She'd been gripping the net so hard her hands hurt and were white at the knuckles. She shivered, and dismounted the net, moving slowly to the backstage exit, checking behind her every other step.

Phillipe The Clown

Phillipe pawed at his face in the mirror. Was that another wrinkle? He pulled a face, patting more clown white onto his skin to cover it up.

He had joined the circus when he was a teenager—a literal 'ran away to join the circus' moment. He had been 16, had finished school with no qualifications, and had figured he had nothing better to do. Gerrent Brothers Circus had been in his town, and he had walked up to Mr Dimitri Gerrent, the ringmaster at the time, and asked for a job.

That was thirty years ago. Starting out in waste management, cleaning animal muck and bins and hay from the circus floor, Phillipe had worked his way up through the ranks. He had no particular skill for sword swallowing, or the trapeze, or stunt bikes—he tried but always came out of it with an injury. And when the law came in that animals were no longer to be part of the circus, he was limited with what he could do. So, he became a clown.

Twenty years ago, there had been a whole troupe of clowns. Big ones, small ones, a group of ten clowns had filled the gaps between acts, but over time, it had become apparent that audiences no longer liked clowns. Many, children and adults alike, found them a little scary. When audience participation dropped, when no child would enter the ring with the clowns, they let the act dwindle, as older clowns retired and no more were taken on.

Eventually, there was only Phillipe left. He had toned down his make-up, taken off the crazy wig and foam nose, and made himself less scary. He still filled the gaps between acts, and with the retirement of the great Dimitri, he was welcomed into a quasi-ringmaster role that had built itself. In a way, he was the central character of the circus, but the acts were the wow factor.

The first two nights had been so quiet. The gang of rowdy men the first evening had turned all the locals against visiting the circus. There were a few groups from neighbouring villages that had turned up, but they were barely half full. It was the last show of the season, too, which meant financially, it would be a hard winter. He sighed and looked around at his caravan. It was looking worse for wear, but it was a case of repairing rather than replacing like he had hoped to.

A bang on his door and hurried voices made his arm jerk a thick back line across his cheek. With a huff, he swiped at the offending mark with the wet towel at his side, and opened the door.

"Phillipe, we've sold out!" Howard and Andreas were panting from running across the camp. "Every ticket. All sold!"

"How? I thought they were boycotting us." Phillipe looked towards the ticket booth, where a crowd had already gathered, but the sold-out banner was taped to the front.

"They've been non-stop all afternoon." Andreas grinned; a sold-out night meant good things for everyone. They could end the season a little better off than anticipated.

"Well, that's great news! Better get on with the show then." Philippe waved them away, the acrobats almost skipping across the camp. Phillipe shook his head in disbelief, then grinned as he spotted the full moon above the big top—bright and round in the twilight sky. It was going to be a good night.

The Gerrent Brothers Circus
The Greatest Show on Earth!

The big top was hot from the number of bodies inside it—even the standing area was full to capacity.

With each act the crowd cheered, shouted and applauded—everyone had their best night. The Bandelerenos had wowed everyone. George had thrown his knives so fast in their final trick, each one landing perfectly along Glinda's outstretched arms. Florence had flown through the air and felt weightless, a thousand eyes following her graceful movements. The acrobats had wowed people as they turned and tossed and tumbled across the ring. And Phillipe had the audience in the palm of his hand with every joke, every trip and fall, and every squirt of the classic water gun flower.

The circus troupe paraded around the ring, every smile genuine as they headed for the final bow—rows of dancers and feathers, the roar of stunt bikes and the stomp of feet as they circled the ring, waving and cheering with the crowd, who had risen to their feet to clap in time with the music. Florence and Fabricio waved from on high in their trapeze seats, swinging back and forth towards each other.

Every face was upturned, glowing, mouths wide with joy. As the music swelled, the performers reached their final positions, waved and bowed. Florence scanned the crowd, each and every audience member looked so happy, it was surely their best crowd yet! Everyone was on their feet, but why were they all moving forward? Had Philippe invited them into the ring? Why would he do that?

There was a scream, and she realised that no one had invited the audience into the ring at all—they were moving en masse towards the performers. A man had grabbed Mary and appeared to be sinking his teeth into her neck. They writhed together, the man's body contorting in ways that couldn't be real; his arms lengthening, fingers sprouting terrifying claws, and a snout housing a mouthful of long, sharp teeth, protruding from his face as he leant his head back and howled—a sound that

221

made Florence's blood freeze. The ring had become a writhing mass of audience members attacking performers, as they transformed into great beasts, howling and screaming below her.

Fabricio swung to the platform and descended into the fray to try and help, but it was no use, there were too many of them. Florence watched in horror as blood pooled beneath bodies, torsos were torn open, and limbs ripped from their sockets. The beasts were wolf-like, and huge. They shredded the flesh with claws and teeth. Hands over her mouth, Florence could do nothing but watch helplessly as the trapeze slowed to a stop in the air above the massacre. She couldn't even see where Fabricio had gone.

A large grey wolf approached the ladder and began to climb up towards the platform. Fabricio's trapeze was not secured, and hung at least 10 meters from the platform—Florence realised that even if she could swing back to her platform, descending the ladder would lead her right into the arms of the wolves circling below her. She had nowhere to go.

Peter had been right. They should have left.

The wolf mounted the platform in seconds, hunched and preparing to spring. Florence kicked her legs to try and swing away but couldn't get momentum quick enough—the wolf leapt towards her, grabbing her in his arms with claws piercing her back. The trapeze snapped from his enormous weight, and for a fleeting moment she was flying again as they plummeted towards the blood-soaked ring floor. The last thing she saw was the pair of startlingly bright blue eyes, framed in fur above a wide open mouth full of teeth.

ON THE EDGE
Scarlett Paige

I stand on the edge. The edge of the dark forest, the edge of time, the edge of death, the edge of desire, and the edge of transformation. Always the edge of something.

I go about day by day conforming, fitting in, being a round peg in a hole that is every shape but round, and always on the edge. I am a woman in a modern world with all the freedoms and constraints afforded to me. I love my husband; he is supportive of all that I do. Well, he is supportive of the me that he knows; the wife, the mother and the checkout girl who loves to bake. He adores me, brings me flowers, gifts and showers me with affection. What more could a girl want? And any other girl but me would be happy. Hell! I would be happy if it weren't for the edge.

It's not that I am constantly unhappy or dissatisfied, it's not that simple. I love my husband and his family, my family, our children, our twin boys. And I like my job, it's not a vocation, but its sociable. And it's not just that I'll never set the world on fire, blaze a trail, or write a bestseller, its more than that. It's a ... well ... a discontentment. No! A discomfort. Or is it a disease? I can no longer tell.

Whatever it is, tonight it is worse than last night, and last night was uncomfortable. Once a month the girls from work get together and go clubbing around the local town and this month's girls' night happens to be tonight! And of course, this time it all began a couple of days ago, and tonight it is unbearable. The only difference this time is that I don't have to feign a last-minute excuse to escape the house, as tonight being girls' night, is at least of some convenience.

Every month it begins with a longing, a yearning, a feeling of wanting something, but what, remains elusive. Then I feel restless, fidgety, and tonight I am once again on the edge. I go through the motions of getting ready. The twins are cuddled up with their father on the sofa watching Disney's Hoodwinked, I kiss them all on the head on route to the shower, shaking my head at the irony.

The shower is warm, and I can feel every drop of water lingering on my skin. The longing inside of me is growing ever stronger, and every last cell in my body is burning with desire. I know I haven't got long, and the intense hunger is getting harder and harder to bear. In a frenzied attempt to quench it I reach between my legs and lean back against the wall of the shower. My fingers work fast, my mind barely has time to keep up with my body, and before I can settle into a fantasy I am gasping for breath, as orgasm grips my body. It is intense, more so than usual. Normally after the long day at work, an orgasm of this magnitude would leave me satisfied and sleepy. But not tonight. Tonight, I am different. Tonight, I am teetering on the edge of all that I am.

My husband has bought me a new dress for tonight, which I put on. It looks good; just the right colour, short and a flattering cut, and any other night I would be delighted, yet tonight, I am not feeling it. Still, I do my make up as normal, curl my long hair before tying it up in a high ponytail, slip on my high heels and head downstairs to kiss my boys before heading out of the front door.

I head out into the night. I have no intention of meeting the girls and I text them that I need an early night, adding a wink emoji. It pays to let them think it's an adult early night, that way they won't check.

The night air is thick and heavy with the scent of the town, yet I can smell the forest drawing nearer with every step. The blood is racing through my veins and my heart throbs uncontrollably with anticipation. The conversations of those I pass ring loudly in my ears and echo around my brain. The forest is close now and my pace quickens as I leave the hustle and bustle of the town behind me. I know the moon is full, I can feel its pull and hear its call. As I enter the forest, I stop and inhale the woodland aroma; dogs and their walkers, the different plants trees and woodland creatures who live there, and of course lovers. The scent of semen, pheromones and female arousal is rife, carried through the forest on the warm summer winds, and it is doing nothing to curb my desire or still my pounding heart. I am on fire, burning at fever pitch.

What will this night bring, I wonder? The anticipation is almost painful. I remove my shoes to feel the cold damp ground beneath my feet and the damp evening grass squashed between my toes. My body has changed, not externally but internally, and my senses are awakened, fuelled by the excitement of possibility. I let my hair down and run barefoot into the forest.

Everything is alive, myself included. I am at one with the world around me, a creature of the night, a child of the universe, driven by the full moon; my senses are heightened, my breath quickened, and my sexual appetite is ravenous, and if there were others like me in the forest I would know, and how much easier the night would pass with a kindred spirit. In fact, I have never met anyone like me, although I have read about them in New Age books.

Modern Lycanthropes who, like psychic vampyres, over the centuries have had their blood lust reduced to an insatiable sexual appetite, which, like their traditional ancestors of myth and legend, is triggered by the full moon. My initial reaction to this was irritation.

I didn't want to be a New Age anything, as those two words alone conjured up rainbow jumpers and reefers! And New Age Lycanthropy conjured up an even more ridiculous image, but once I learned more, I gradually became more accepting. Besides, the throbbing pulse and burning fever coursing through my veins, coupled with the overwhelming sexual desire, made it all a bit hard to dismiss. I can only assume if I exist then so do others, and I often wonder how that would play out. Maybe, just maybe, one day I'll find out, but not today.

Right now, I see a man in the distance. In truth I smell him long before I see him. He is smartly dressed, a businessperson perhaps. He catches a glimpse of me in the moonlight bare footed and with windswept hair. I can smell that he is overcome by desire, and I can also smell that he has not long climaxed, although the female scent eludes me, so I can only assume he is single. At least for tonight.

I feel control slipping away as I walk up to him, he begins to make small talk, but it hurts my ears. I press against him so close he has to kiss me, and I lead him deep into the forest where I initiate the consummation of our unholy, somewhat animalistic union. The bulge I can feel against me says he is interested, so for now he is mine, at least for the next few moments. My pillow talk is brief but profound and will affect his life from here on in. For him, this may well be a life changing moment, although I will not remember my words, which are far beyond the usual sexual word play. I can feel him inside of me, still growing with every thrust and I moan beneath him as I reach the brink of orgasm, and here, where others whisper, 'fuck me', I whisper racing tips, business strategies, global objectives, even lottery numbers.

My profound magical whispers are subliminal. I always wonder why they remember the words and I nothing, but perhaps it is better that way. I will take many lovers tonight, both male and female. I will pleasure them equally working my tongue in and out of the women and feeling the full extent of many men. Inside I am howling, and my howling is their voice of reason, lady luck, long awaited answers. Call it what you will.

My moments of lust have changed so many lives as over the years; I have seduced businessmen and women, musicians, artists and writers. I am the changeling, the wolf in slut's clothing, the virgin, the mother and whore. I am a modern lycanthrope ruled by the call of the moon and lost in the depths of the night. I am she who loves, and through my desires, magick occurs.

And tonight, as much as I am caught up in the madness of the moment, lost in darkness and desire, I am still on the edge; I am on the edge of the town, the edge of a new day, the edge of satisfaction and the edge of conformity. As I said, I am always on the edge!

IN MY
DARKEST HOURS
Annerose Weiler

In my darkest hours
I am in a haze.
Day and night
Month after month
Away from home:
Having lost so much
My mind is bent to the ground.
My heart is raw, so raw
I've never known before.
My sense of 'I'The human me
Whittled to a speck.

What if there were a thing
Like werewolf at night
And I were cursed
That once in a while
I would grow some fur
Turn into a mighty beast.

A tiger.

And run to you on all four paws
Thirsty for blood
Hungry for flesh
Craving a bite of your heart.

How I would pounce!

If I woke the following day
Down on the ground
In human form
Would I remember?
Bewildered and shocked?
Or simply rise
And lick my lips.